THE FIREKEEPER

Michael A. Susko

AllrOneofUs Publishing
Baltimore, Md & Huntsville, Al

While every precaution has been taken in the preparation of this book, the publisher assumes no responsibility for errors or omissions, or for damages resulting from the use of the information contained herein.

THE FIREKEEPER

First edition. November 26, 2019.

ISBN: 978-1393526469

Written by Michael A. Susko.

To the unnoticed who fight spiritual battles so that our
community may live.

CHAPTER ONE
KIN SPIRITS OF THE FIRE

LET THE CHILD LIVE, the youth heard in his mind. It was a moment of joy before his fear gathered. It was the dead of night, and the fire had burnt down to red embers. Moeslet was waking, as if out of a trance.

He spoke to the fire, struggling to stay awake. "I will bring you back to life! I will stir you and coax you back."

Beyond the reach of its light was a dark, half-shaped thing, looking at him. There was something else too, like an enormous cat, but it flickered away. Maybe it went to the mountains where it lived in the shadows. The dark spirit that remained was content to stir around the edges of light. It did not seem to want to bother him tonight.

Moeslet got up, his body aching. He moved long bones further into the fire and blew hard until the flames leapt.

"Be gone," he shouted, waving a flaming bone and, to his surprise, the unnamed thing left. Still, the spirit might return in the dark, and Moeslet needed to stay awake. Some long bones, already cracked for their marrow, were in reserve. The kin were sleeping, except for a guard who stood out a way. Moeslet longed for a human voice, but heard only an occasional owl hooting.

If the spirit had left, Moeslet still had an enemy to face. It crept over his face and took hold of his eyes. He shook his head, splashed water on his face, and walked about. But the moment he sat down, the enemy returned. Moeslet needed stronger medicine, so he turned to Fire and touched a small coal. The pain leapt up his arm. The burning lingered, but Moeslet had slain the enemy.

Day came, Moeslet's time to sleep. For a few drowsy moments, he would hear the screams of playing children. The kin spoke fast, and he couldn't make out all the words. But he knew slower words that they didn't. He knew the words of Fire, which spoke to him.

The men of the day would become busy doing things he could not do well--knapping stones, preparing skins, and hunting. But Moeslet knew how to keep a fire alive, to harden a stick with fire, and change the colors of stones. Still, those his own age would make fun of him, for he didn't do the usual man things and had a lameness in one leg. He was alone.

Moeslet was also alone because he had no parents. His birth had taken the life of his mother, and a wild beast had killed his father. It was the way of the kin that everyone had a use and a gift, and his was tending the night fire. Everyone depended on him; but everyone, it seemed, took him for granted.

A few childhood friends had not forgotten they once played together. Sometimes, they would watch the fire with him late into the night. Leola was his favorite, for they used to go on adventures along the stream. She knew the ways of water and would show him the homes of frogs and water birds. When she grew older, her father discouraged her from playing with him. *"Those who do not hunt cannot have a woman,"* was a saying of the kin.

It was true, Moeslet could not kill, for he had not the strength or desire. If he saw an animal, he sensed its spirit and could not kill it. He realized this when he tended a dying bird once. The male hunters did not understand, for they thought nothing could be gained from saving a wounded animal.

So the day would pass, and Moeslet would sleep before waking for his night tending. Each day, the kin would leave him wood and bones, for such was his lameness that he gathered only kindling.

Leola sometimes visited him in secret. She talked about the things of the day—the sun, the clouds, the fish in the stream, and the soaring birds. Leola was curious about fire, for she had seen Moeslet talking to it. She always had questions. "What was the fire's mood last night? When there isn't much left for Fire to eat, what do you do? When it goes down to embers, how do you get it to rise from its hiding place?"

Leola had so many questions, so many words. *Yes, we should be together,* Moeslet felt, *but it can't be.* It was a deep pain that he had not the power to claim her. True, he had power from Fire, but it was not to be used against the kin. It was the way of things. She was of the day and the many, and he was of the night and alone.

Once on a chilly night, her father had found Leola and him, their arms wrapped around each other. Her father had struck him. They were no longer children, nor could they be something more.

Leola agreed too easily to her father's demand, he felt. Moeslet knew they could be happy together; and he knew, too, that she did not know this. Leola thought she just enjoyed being around the fire with him and the words that rose in her. He didn't always make out the meaning of her words, but he liked to hear them flowing.

"Tell me what the fire is saying," she asked one night.

How does she know that the fire speaks? Moeslet wondered. It was something that he had learned only after many months of being with the fire through dark and cold nights. Fire could speak, but its words were deep and secret. Fire had words, but they were not easily revealed.

Leola talked and asked easily, and as she was his only real friend among the kin, he would answer. He wondered if Fire would become angry. Would it leap out and try to claim her? But Fire did not dislike her, for it did not become moody, but burned just as truly when she was around. Still, Moeslet did not tell her all. One had to be cautious with Fire, for it could suddenly change and kill.

Fire had its fears, as well. Once, when driving rain blew into the cave's mouth, the fire had died. The kin tried to save it, but there was no bringing it back. Cold followed, then sickness and death. No one knew why the fire had left them. Had someone made it angry? Had a powerful spirit sought its life?

Some blamed the Firekeeper and said there should be a new one. Moeslet wondered if he would survive. It was because he cared for the fire at night that families shared their food with him. Would a new Firekeeper let him sleep nearby and share his food? It would be hard to be apart from Fire, who had been his friend and teacher, the one closest to him.

It might have gone differently, but an elder had argued for him. "Let him remain, for he is close to the ways of fire. The cold and dark sometimes win, but the fire will come back to him."

A few days later, fire fell from the sky, and a hunter brought back a burning branch.

"What do you think the fire is saying?" Leola asked him one evening, using a stick to toy with its embers.

"Fire is yawning. It's sleepy but is happy to be alive."

"No, it's saying, 'I burn bright because I have plenty of fresh bones to eat. I will kill the dark tonight!'"

Fire did not seem to be angry at this and didn't leap her way.

Moeslet gazed at the face he had known for so long, yet saw anew. *It must mean we're kin spirits of Fire and that we are meant for each other...*

CHAPTER TWO
A DAY OF HUNTING AND HIDING

WHEN THE WEATHER WAS hot and the fire had plenty of fuel, Moeslet would sometimes sleep through the night, having no fear the fire would extinguish. He must have slept long this night, for the camp was already stirring when he woke. Leola's dark hair shimmered by the fire. Poking his side, she kidded Moeslet, "A Firekeeper who sleeps through the night and into the day?"

When his own words failed him, Moeslet drew upon sayings. "When the sun is strong, the fire keeps itself."

He did not reveal that Fire had spoken to him, leaving him free to venture out this day. Why the fire sometimes released him, he was not sure. He gathered that it knew this day would be warm, clear, and windless. He looked up at the sky with traces of cloud and smiled. "The day is mine. The fire is content to be by itself."

Leola's smile held some mischief. "Yes, Fire is happy." She stirred it with a stick, pushed embers to its center, and then threw the stirring stick into the middle.

A young hunter named Ishman, who had sat down across from the fire, overheard their words. "Does this mean that Moeslet will go out with the hunters today? We will be hunting the Long Hairs. But I forget it is too much for Moeslet to see blood and death."

"No, it is not!" was all Moeslet could think to say. He wondered, *was it for this reason that Fire had released him*? It was rare that the kin hunted big game. A mammoth herd must be near the canyon, where they could make a kill.

"I will tell the others you are coming," Ishman prodded. "I know you are tired of killing wood, bones, and dirt in the fire." With the latter, he was referring to earthen balls that Moeslet would throw in the fire and watch burst.

Moeslet stared at Ishman, almost a challenge, for he knew why Ishman was pushing him. Ishman liked Leola, and he wanted to show that he could hunt and that Moeslet couldn't.

The Firekeeper wiped the soot from his hands and stood up. "I will go. I do not fear the mammoth."

It was true. Moeslet had no fear of any living animal. What he feared was the *spirit* of a slain animal. But Ishman's taunts had overridden this fear. He no longer wanted to be called a weak changeling who could not bear to see death. Boys much younger than he had seen a mammoth kill.

It surprised Ishman, who took his leave.

Not really thinking, and because Moeslet thought the day would be different from this, he asked Leola. "Will you go with me?"

She laughed. "A woman on a hunt? If we bleed, it would keep the animals away. But you don't know of such things." Lowering her voice, she added, "After the hunt, I will show you something."

Moeslet's look questioned, and she answered, "By the stream where we used to play, I know of an animal's secret hiding place."

Moeslet wondered, *could two things happen on the same day? The fire somehow knew....*

He acted as if he wasn't so pleased. "After the hunt, I will go with you."

Her eyes flickered. "Don't forget. You are not of the day, and the day has its ways."

Moeslet nodded. The day always surprised him.

A hunt was mostly watching and waiting. A dozen men lay hidden above a canyon trap, seeking to draw the mammoth inside with sounds and food. Then they would hurl spears and rocks down upon the creature until it died. Moeslet knew that much.

Still, he feared to see the death, if they succeeded. The creature's spirit would leave in a rage, and it would try to lay its hand over one of them. He had felt the dying spirits of smaller animals and knew the danger. To extinguish a large, bright flame would not be easy. It was part of his gift, to see things that people of the day did not, and he wondered why.

Taumax, the shaman, was not pleased to hear that the Firekeeper was going on the hunt, for losing him would endanger the group's welfare. When he found out that Moeslet would not carry a weapon and watch from a distance, he did not protest.

The hunters, along with the shaman, followed the stream toward the mountain, and then veered to the left toward a canyon. They gathered branches from the ends of trees with buds and flowers. They were not here to build a fire, but to put one out.

The sun was waning when a large, male mammoth walked into their trap. At first, he was slow, extending his trunk curiously. The hunters were downwind, but something made him hesitate. The mound of plants placed at the canyon's end and the sounds of mating attracted him.

When sticks pierced the beast's flank, and blood flowed, Moeslet half closed his eyes. The creature's screaming rent the air, and the Firekeeper felt a pressure against his face, almost causing him to turn his head. He knew others would notice, so he kept watching as the hunters struck and wounded the animal to death.

Descending to the canyon floor, the hunters now thrust at the animal up close. The mammoth fell to its knees, and Ishman, the boldest, struck the mammoth from the front.

The great beast gasped and blood gushed from its mouth. Its time had come.

Moeslet saw the spirit come out, dark, strong and raging. It wanted to strike someone with a curse and cause an untimely death. The shaman made a ritual sign and uttered words of protection. The spirit passed over the circle of hunters but hovered on the fringes, hungry. It lingered over a small boy who had been watching his father from a distance. It was about to strike.

No! cried the Firekeeper from his voice within. *Come my way!*

The invited spirit hurried toward him, a wind stirring in its wake. Fearsome, the spirit questioned, "You called me? You would be marked?"

Moeslet bowed his head, seeking to appease it. "Come at night, and I will tend to you."

"No," ordered another voice, the shaman's. How could Moeslet forget he was there? Holding his staff, Taumax spoke powerful words of departing. The spirit was not so easily appeased, for it desired to inflict a death for a death, and it sensed a claim within its grasp.

But Taumax was experienced. The spirit of the shaman leapt like a panther and fought the mammoth's spirit. The only sign of fighting was a cloud of dust twisting over the ground. A few moments later, Taumax had won. The shaman sat down, exhausted.

Later, the shaman raised his face, angry and puzzled. "Why do you meddle with spirit things? Why would you take on what you know little about? The spirit could have come at night and slain you!"

Moeslet had no answer. "I saw the boy and ..."

"Perhaps you see things. But why draw a dangerous spirit to yourself? You would endanger all the kin?"

Moeslet did not know how to explain an action that now looked foolish.

Taumax considered for a moment, as if seeing the boy anew. "Perhaps you should know a few shaman things. But I have an apprentice already, and your role is given. For the one who keeps the fire alive, keeps us all alive."

That's just a saying, Moeslet wanted to reply. *It brings me no glory, just smoke and darkness --and no friend but Fire.*

"The fire speaks to me," Moeslet revealed, although there had not been a question.

"It does...? Of course. You keep it alive."

Taumax considered more. "Come to me when the moon is full each month, and I will teach you a few things."

Was it for this that Fire wanted me to go out into the day? It was good news, even though he would not be a shaman's apprentice. Moeslet would learn some things of power in case of need. He knew Taumax had shown a few minor things to others. But no other kin, except Leola, had bothered to teach Moeslet. He wondered if the fire would be jealous and decided to ask it later.

The day is already filled with wonderful things, and there's something more.

"Did you help kill the mammoth? Did you stick a spear into its heart?" Leola teased, knowing he would not do such a thing. They followed the stream as it meandered from the mountains and widened into a flowering meadow.

Moeslet, his expression suddenly serious, turned to face her. "I saw its spirit flee."

"Oh, yes. You see spirit things... What did the fleeing spirit say?"

"Angry spirits speak little," Moeslet lied. "I would have liked to ask it something."

"Then ask, and I will speak for it."

Leola was crazy like that, thinking she could know the words of a slain beast. Moeslet looked about, wondering if the spirit was still present, but the shaman had surely slain it in a second death.

Moeslet nodded, knowing her words would come, even when there should be no words. They came to a moss bed by the stream, screened by beautiful leaves. It was a cool place. He had never been so far away from the fire and for so long. They sat down, and she gazed right into his eyes.

"The animal would say," Leola began, "Why did you take my home of flesh and bone? Have you left me to be eaten by other beasts, and to be scattered on the ground? Where will I find a new home? Since you have done this to me, you must help me find a new home."

She was talking secrets, not the whole secret, but chasing after it.

"Enough of spirits!" Moeslet suddenly insisted, surprised at his anger.

Leola wasn't upset, and she didn't seem to care about talking anymore. *Why are we waiting?* he wondered.

Moeslet broke the silence. "So, where is this animal's hiding place?"

"Silly boy, it's here." And she kissed him.

It was different; it was changing. Moeslet had seen others do this, but he had not guessed what it would be like.

It was just a few moments, but it left Moeslet in a swoon. Had Leola done this as a teacher, or so she had thought? Still, it left Moeslet happy. Today had been a big day for him, for he had learned two things. *Both shamans and women have the power of changing.*

CHAPTER THREE
THE HUNTERS OF HUMANS

A FEW YEARS PASSED, and winter's time had come again, when nights were long and cold, and the Firekeeper struggled to keep awake. It was a time of fear, when blankets of cold descended upon all, and the mouth of the cave darkened, as if there was no other light in the world. The unseen cave walls kept some heat within.

Sometimes the eyes of others would wake and look at the Firekeeper. He learned not to look back, but he could feel their eyes. When Moeslet felt Leola look his way, he would flick his fire stick and shower sparks. She was a grown woman now, and the hunter Ishman would soon take her as his.

The winter was hard, for the herds had not come their way, and there was little food. The kin knew it was a time of danger. Some became sick, including Leola, and Moeslet worried.

There was another danger. From the other side of the mountains, bands of those who hungered for humans would come and hunt. The Fearsome Ones rarely challenged the kin, for they were many and adept at throwing spears and stones. But sometimes these hunters of humans would take one—a sick person left unprotected, a child who wandered too far, or one who slept apart.

Moeslet was glad that the kin did not kill their own for food, for he could not have borne a human's spirit departing, their outrage at their house being eaten. He did not know if there was any ritual that could keep them safe from a human spirit.

The winter continued to press, and there was talk of doing more to survive. In years long ago, when the hunger had grown great, the kin had taken one of their own for food. They had decided that it was acceptable if the need was great enough, and the food was taken from one who died bravely. The shaman would judge the death and whether the offering was acceptable.

The group's faces and bodies had become lean, and the hunters talked of killing one from another troop. Taumax held firm, saying that was not their way. So the kin waited and became weaker.

Despairing, Moeslet asked Fire, "Why don't the animals come to us? Why must we talk of killing one of our own or from another group? How are we going to survive?"

The fire did not answer the question right away. "Feed me another bone," it said.

Moeslet gave a large bone, already scoured for marrow.

"Better," said Fire.

"Why are you fed and we are not?" Moeslet persisted, "We are your Keeper, but who keeps us?" The fire liked riddles like this.

Its flames crackled brighter. "You are kept, although you little know your Keeper."

Moeslet, who usually took his time answering, fired back, "If we have a Keeper, how come we have not been given food? Am I not feeding you, so you can stay alive?"

The fire blazed higher. "Yes, you are a flame that must be fed, too. Hasn't it been so for all these years?"

"Who gives us food now? We suck the dry bones before we give them to you."

"Someone will die and the kin will survive," Fire revealed.

The fire had finally answered the question. It always did. The Firekeeper was happy and sad. The kin would survive, but someone would die. Invariably, the fire was right when it foretold the future.

Moeslet became anxious, as Leola was fighting sickness.

"No, not her," revealed Fire.

So the kin had their hunger fed, and it happened as Fire had said. In the heart of winter, there was a battle with the hunters of humans. Before dawn, the kin's guard had sounded the alarm. The Hunters attacked fiercely, swinging their sticks and pressing the kin against the fire. One kin was pierced and fell. Amid the confusion, Moeslet bent over the wounded man with flames around them. Then Moeslet felt a blow to his head, and all became black.

When the Firekeeper woke the next day, the shaman was conducting a ritual over the bones of a hunter. His flesh had been removed, and his bones cleaned and dusted with red ochre. The bones were arranged around a smooth-shaped rock.

Taumax threw a bison skin over the rock and declared, "The bison gives life. The warrior has changed into the bison."

What the fire said has come true, Moeslet realized. *The kin will survive the winter.*

"What happened?" asked the Firekeeper.

"No man touched you," a hunter answered. "You must have fainted and hit your head."

"It was good that you did not die," another added, "for only one who dies bravely can be offered."

Ishman laughed. "You were in the fire, but your friend did not burn you. It protects the one who feeds it."

Moeslet was angry, but what could he say? Why was he weak and left to fight spirit things?

Something more had happened that night, and memory flooded Moeslet's mind. He had come back to consciousness and had seen a dark spirit come to take a life. The Firekeeper had faced it alone. He knew there was little or no chance to survive this battle, such was the strength of this spirit. He had called on the shaman for help but received no answer.

Moeslet once asked the shaman about the spirit who came in the dead of winter. Taumax had looked out into the night and said, "You need not concern yourself with this matter." The spirit had left on its own, and there had been no danger.

But this night, Moeslet battled the spirit. He was not alone, for Fire had seen it too. Whatever it was, the fire did not seem to fear it, but neither did Fire fight it. Still, Fire knew that if its keeper died, it might die too. So that night, the fire blazed higher than from just wood and bones. Fire drew upon a power greater than itself and did not claim him when he fell into it.

Moeslet remembered another thing: the name of the spirit. Fire had spoken its name, *Obtwust*. One must know a spirit's name to fight it, but Moeslet sensed there was no way to fight such a powerful spirit.

Moeslet had but a faint memory of what happened next. He had stayed awake and spoke to distract the spirit until dawn. He had not the strength or power to wound it, much less kill it—only to delay it, until the sun rose, for then the spirit had the habit of leaving.

The night was long and cold, and Moeslet's energy drained. The fire had become small, flickering embers. It felt like the end, his last night of life, for he knew no more words to delay the spirit which took lives.

Yet, somehow, he found more. Thinking back, Moeslet did not remember what he said. He only remembered darkness and cold, and the night spirit hovering.

Then more memory came. The kin were close to death, for the *Obtwust* wanted to take them all, and it almost did. Its plan was to crush Fire, then enter deeper into the cave, and put the kin into a death slumber. The Fearsome Ones would come and finish its work.

That night the fire almost died, for the *Obtwust* had cast a spell of cold and darkness, and there was no more wood or bones. The Firekeeper, his head throbbing, gathered and put in twigs, leaves, dirt, even rocks. He tried to think of more words, but his mind was blank and numb from the cold.

The fire was almost out. Why was the spirit attacking again? Then Moeslet thought of Leola, who always spoke, even when she didn't know what she was saying. So he spoke a few Leola, sing-song words which he hoped would shoot an arrow into the heart of the spirit. The Obtwust was not fazed, however. It just waited. It became so dark and cold that Moeslet felt the rawness of death against his face. He had no more words left. He would die.

CHAPTER FOUR
A MID-WINTER BIRTHING

WHEN THE FIREKEEPER woke, his head ached fiercely, and his body was faint from exhaustion. A sharp pain lodged in his chest. The kin said it was from the fall, but Moeslet knew he had gained this hurt from another battle. Still, the spirit had only glanced him before leaving upon the dawn's first flickering. The spirit had left, but not without a price.

So Moeslet fought this dark spirit-thing and did not tell anyone. Who would believe him? And as time passed, it seemed like a dream that happened in a faraway time and land.

Spring came, bleak winter days were far from everyone's thoughts, and the plants and animals brought food. Sometimes the events of deep winter were remembered, about how one had given his life so they all could live. The story-teller ended on a note, which caused everyone to laugh. "Moeslet was there too. He fought against a rock by the fire, and the rock won. Luckily, the fire, his friend, protected him as he slept."

Moeslet remained silent, knowing he shouldn't feel shame. Yet anger rose in him. *They'll see. Next winter I will not fight the dark spirit nor delay its wishes. I will even tell it which one to slay. It will be Ishman!*

Or maybe I will just let the fire go out. The kin might survive; they might not. Let another keep the fire and see if he can face the Obtwust!

Seeing his pain, Leola came to him. "You are still the one who keeps the fire," she said, taking his hand. "You stay awake and face the darkness and cold alone. If no one else thanks you, I do." She hugged him.

Did Leola know of his struggle? No, she could not know about his battling this spirit. Once, he had tried to tell her, but she took it as a story. How much he wanted to share with her and hear her flow of words about the *Obtwust*.

Just then, Ishman came and led her away. He said nothing, for he knew the Firekeeper was no threat. He also knew that Moeslet had two friends: the fire and Leola, and he did not want to anger either.

Moeslet's anger subsided, and he decided he would keep tending the fire. *I will even stay awake on the long winter night and face the spirit again, for I love Leola, the one I can never have.*

Moeslet looked at the fire, which burned bright and true. "At least we are together."

It seemed Fire burned brighter for a moment. It said no words, but its flames sent a warmth through him.

Moeslet saw more of the fire and less of Leola. He became restless and stayed up some during the day. The kin wondered, "When does the Firekeeper sleep? Does he want to know the ways of the night and the day?"

Moeslet smiled. The children came to him, and he would tell them stories. One time, he referred to the *Obtwust*, although he didn't use its name. Two or three looked intently and seemed to understand.

One time, Moeslet told a long story that would be shared with an apprentice of a Firekeeper. He did so to study the children's faces and see who might come after him. Using a drawing stick, Moeslet helped the children follow the story.

"At the beginning the world was gloomy, and humans lived in darkness. There were no animals or plants, so the world had no food."

Moeslet drew wavy lines and floating stick figures. "Yet there was warmth in the darkness, and the people lived like spirits floating.

"Then a time came when people saw a circle of light, too painful for their eyes to look directly upon." Moeslet drew a circle with rays and a shut eye. "While they were attracted to the light, they feared it might extinguish them. One of their own, a youth named Olanda, dared to seek the circle of light. After a long and perilous journey, he finally reached the ends of the world. He extended his arms and basked in the light." Moeslet drew rays around a stick figure.

"When Olanda returned, his face and body glowed, and at first the people feared him. Olanda told them that the glow was but a small part of what he had seen. The people became fascinated by the light, and after it diminished, they said to him, 'Go and bring us back this light again.'

"So the youth returned to the land of the circle light and discovered more. He saw trees that raised their limbs to the light and fabulous creatures that flew in the sky. The light orb receded, and he followed the light for days until he came upon the orb of fire atop a mountain. It was too much light and heat to approach. How, he wondered, could he bring back some of this light to his people?

"Olanda got used to the heat and light and came nearer to the orb. Still, he could not come close enough to touch it. The idea came to him, to put a branch into the fire.

"When he tried to tear off a branch, however, the tree screamed, 'Why rip off my limb?'

'My people live in darkness and want this light,' Olanda answered.

'Why not use your own limb?'

'I cannot use mine, for I will die.'

'You cannot bring light into your world without cost.'

"Olanda left downcast, but he was still bright from being so near the fire. The glow lasted longer than before, but when it wore off, the people again demanded that he go back. 'Bring us a flame so we can have this light always, or do not return.'

"Once more, Olanda went through the opening and stood before the fire. 'My people ask for life and light.'

"The fiery orb spoke, 'Put your hand into my side so you may know me.'

"Olanda wondered if this would cause his death, but he could not return without the flame.

"The youth put his hand in the fire and the pain made him one with the flame. And in this dying, he understood the fire. Pulling out his seared hand, flames still issued from his fingertips. So, in this way, fire came into the world.

"Olanda's hand healed, but every year at the time he had taken the fire, it seared as if it were burning again. That is why, to this day, each Keeper is tested by Fire."

Moeslet searched the children's faces. Three had followed the story closely, although they could not comprehend its full meaning. He would need one of them, to not only keep the fire, but to battle the Spirit of the Long Night.

How could I wish such a life upon a young one? he wondered. *It would be a curse: to be alone, to fight such battles and not be known, and to have Fire as your only friend.*

Moeslet realized that whoever he chose, he must be able to *see*. No one so far had shown this gift, but one or two might as they grew older.

Not long after, Moeslet asked Fire, "Who will tend you, when I am gone?"

Fire avoided answering. "Where are you going?"

"No one knows their time of leaving. One day, something will happen, and I will be gone."

"Yes, one day you will become as a flame."

"The elders say we become a star. But a spirit in the sky cannot tend you. You will need a living one from among the kin."

The fire brooded, not wanting to accept that things could change.

Moeslet insisted. "One day there will be a new Keeper, one who can tend you and face the dark spirit. The New One must be able to *see* and fight the spirit, lest it kill all the kin."

The fire kept silent.

Moeslet returned to the first question. "You taught me how to be your Keeper. Will you help me teach another?"

The fire did not like the thought of losing its Keeper. Its answer surprised Moeslet. "Why do you worry about things after you are gone? When I die, it will be like all fire has died."

"My people will not die! You must teach the new Keeper to tend you and to fight the dark spirit."

"There is a way," Fire finally said.

"Tell me."

The fire was silent for a while yet. It did not give up its secrets easily.

Moeslet waited, but he had hope, for Fire had said, *There is a way.* He must be patient, for such was Fire's way. He would keep feeding it and bear with its long silences. Then, one day, Fire would answer. Hopefully it would not take too long, for the fire had its own sense of time. Sometimes it would answer so much later that Moeslet would forget his question.

"What was the question to this answer?" he would ask.

Fire would come as close to laughing as a fire could. Sometimes it told him the question, sometimes not. But Moeslet would not forget *this* question.

Time changed during Moeslet's nights of watching. He entered a deeper time and saw hidden things amid the changing. It seemed that Fire had gained an eye, that it watched something that lay beyond it. So they were not alone. He was with the fire and something more.

Leola was to be joined with Ishman this spring. She had not forgotten Moeslet and would sometimes talk to him.

"Your eyes are bright," she said one day. "Can you tell me what makes the light in your eyes?"

Moeslet had no words for the answer.

"Do you not see the sun at night?" she asked. "Does not the fire become your light at night and let you touch the night spirits?"

How does she know to say this? Moeslet wondered. *Leola is making things up, but it seems a spirit is guiding her.*

Leola suddenly hugged him and declared, "I will always love you. But I must follow the ways of the kin. We are still like *one*, and we will not forget each other."

Moeslet was lost for words, and tears came to his eyes. He wanted to shout, "I should have you as my woman! I am a great warrior, for I fight the dark and the great Spirit of Winter's Long Night!"

He realized it would sound silly. He did not look like a person of power, and no one recognized him as such. Only the fire knew, and sometimes a child might believe one of his stories. Besides, he could not tell, for the fire had said that it would draw away his powers. Moeslet needed to save as much power as possible, if he and the kin were to survive.

"I will protect you, even if you be with Ishman," Moeslet promised.

Leola looked puzzled. "Yes, you tend the fire, and it protects us." She walked away.

The seasons passed, and Moeslet readied to face winter and the *Obtwust* again. But this time, the long night passed without incident. Maybe the spirit visited other peoples, or maybe it planned to take more lives the following year. You could never tell what the *Obtwust* would do.

Spring came again. Leola and Ishman were now partners, and Moeslet tended the fire. It seemed that nothing had changed, and that everything had.

In the early summer, Leola was with child. She would have her time of birthing in the winter. She requested Moeslet help the midwife keep the fire for the birthing chamber in the cave. In this place, the heat of the daughter fire would be strong, and the flow of cave air would take the smoke away.

It was not usual to have the Firekeeper help with a lesser fire for birthing. That would usually fall to the midwife's assistant. However, a lame male such as Moeslet was not considered strongly male or female in the realm of things. So the midwife named Tohna had made the request. Perhaps she sensed that extra skill would be needed this winter.

Still, for Moeslet to tend two fires in winter would be challenging. A newborn could more easily die then, so Moeslet would have to be careful. He performed the ritual of making a new fire, asking Fire's permission to make an infant one.

At first, the mother fire had resisted. "You take my flame and then will kill it?"

"It is for a new life of the kin to enter this world."

Fire was silent, brooding. Then it said something that verged on human, "Do you think I want to lose my young?"

Moeslet found anger rising in him, for he had no young and would never have any. But the fire would not understand this, and Moeslet let it pass. Was there not the saying, *Be content with what is given?* It was good enough that he could help Leola bring a child into the world. When Moeslet realized that the mother fire had said neither yes nor no, he took the flame.

The time of birthing drew near. Moeslet sprinkled the ground with red ochre to prepare the bed of the birthing mother. First, the ochre had been darkened by fire to give it the strength of fire. Then the shaman added his blessing, and the ochre was cast, making a circle of protection.

The rituals were finished in time. Two days later Leola's birthing contractions began, the time of peril. Although it was many days before the long night, the *Obtwust* appeared, perhaps sensing opportunity.

Moeslet had foreseen this and was ready. He felt the hunger of the hovering presence until he could bear the silence no more. Moeslet spoke ritual words and added his own. *"A new life can come into the world, if the spirits allow it.* Will you take a life that has not seen the world?"

That would have been enough to ward off a wandering night spirit, but the *Obtwust* was not so easily put off. Perhaps it remembered that it had not visited the previous year.

The *Obtwust* seemed in no mood to talk, and Moeslet realized that this brought peril. The spirit's presence felt large as a mountain, ready to fall and take the child.

Moeslet blurted out his feelings, forgetting how risky that was. "You must not take a child from the one I love!"

The *Obtwust* spoke with sudden anger. "Why do you tell me this? Can you order me who to take? It is not your child!"

The Obtwust is cruel, thought Moeslet, but he mustn't let his pain answer. He pieced two sayings together. *"The spirits give and take lives as they will. But when a life comes, it is a bright time.*

The *Obtwust* darkened. It wanted more than sayings. "This birth comes near the time when I claim life. Why do you tell me of one you love, who carries a child which is not yours?"

It had been a mistake to tell of his love, Moeslet realized, but he could not take back his words. He tried to control the emotions surging through him. *"It is not for the living to choose who lives among them."* Still, his safest words were sayings.

The *Obtwust's* anger only rose. "I think I will take both mother and child."

Moeslet fought back his panic. He could not bear the thought of losing Leola, even if she was not his. The spirit was demanding that

Moeslet use his own words, but he could not think of any. He thought of Leola, to say something for her life. It came out as a half groan, a cry of pain. Even though it was not a word, the spirit heard, and it left—but not before saying, "I will return the next night."

Moeslet could hardly sleep that day. He had felt the *Obtwust's* strength and realized that when it returned, it would take a life. This had happened before. New life coming into the world was always risky. Why did Leola's child have to come at the worst time?

The midwife sensed something was wrong, and that there was special danger to the child. *"Protect the mother first,"* she told Moeslet. "For the mother can bear a child again."

Did the midwife somehow know? Moeslet wondered. He looked hard at Tohna, who was both old and wise. *Maybe she can see at the time of childbearing. Maybe she knows about the Obtwust. Could it not be? New lives come from the spirit world, and the midwife guides their entrance.* So the midwife had revealed to him one of their basic rules. Still, it was a hard rule that allowed a little one to die.

Moeslet had permission to follow the rule, and the midwife, he gathered, would help him. A young and small spirit of a newly formed human could be fearsome and bring trouble when loosed, however. The unlived life would scream, and those around it would be pierced by the scream.

Moeslet readied to resist the spirit. He knew its question would return, and he had thought his answer. Still, it was not the first response that worried him, but the ones that followed, which must come quickly and without fear.

In the deep of night, the *Obtwust* came as promised. Its presence was powerful, able to take any kin it wanted. Soon after, he heard screams from the pain of birthing. Leola's time had come, but Moeslet could not let that distract him. He steadied himself, looking into the infant fire, which didn't know any words.

The *Obtwust* hovered over all, and Moeslet sensed something was wrong. The spirit seemed to ignore Moeslet and to have forgotten its question. What should Moeslet say then? He must speak and delay the spirit until light. The *Obtwust* had already shown that it could override a saying if it wanted.

"You have given a question," started Moeslet. "And I have an answer."

"Questions come and go," the *Obtwust* deigned to reply, "and if not answered in time, they are no more."

These words were both good and bad. The question seemed to be gone, but the *Obtwust* had spoken. The midwife, glancing up from her tending Leola, seemed to sense the spirit. And among the embers, the infant fire was only a few flames, under the weight of the dark spirit.

Moeslet knew he must use his wits, but he was not a person of wits. Nothing came to mind. He only knew that he mustn't lose Leola, the one who always had words. It was surely a mistake to show weakness again, but they were the only words he could think, so he mixed them with the midwives' rule.

"I love Leola, and I will fight for her life. If you must take one, take the small one and not the mother."

The *Obtwust* was silent, dark and brooding. It had already moved over the birthing Leola, ready to lower its hand. The infant fire was crushed. Moeslet felt his energy draining, his strength leaving, and the midwife's too. It was the time of testing, weighing... Leola's screaming had stopped. Her face was cold and blue from a death pall.

Just as he felt that Leola's life would leave her, Moeslet heard the midwife. "Take the child and leave as you have first asked!" Her command was imperious, brokering no other response.

Moeslet knew the Obtwust did not have to obey. Yet the spirit said, "So I have asked," and in an instant, it was gone.

The *Obtwust*, however, took the child and its spirit too. It absorbed the child's screaming, and a lifeless child was born into the world. Leola woke and cried amid the bleeding.

CHAPTER FIVE
THE NEW FIREKEEPER

EVEN WHEN YOUNG, A Firekeeper could gain an apprentice. The kin rarely lived to have gray hair, for death could come suddenly and in varied ways. Leola had a brush with death and had lived. Moeslet visited her as she recovered, although Ishman did not like it. The hunter thought the Firekeeper had brought her bad luck, as some had said.

Moeslet longed for a human friend, so why not ask for a helper? He went to the elders, who decided things, and asked for an apprentice. Under the full moon they had gathered by a great oak whose ancient roots broke through the ground, leaving upturned stones and places to sit. In their midst was a large smooth stone, which was polished from the touch of many feet and hands. It was there that the one who spoke stood.

Moeslet's turn came. "I must teach another before I become old." He already had a boy in mind, someone who showed promise in *seeing*, one who talked of his dreams, and stayed up late. But the boy was also adept at other things and would become a good hunter, so the Council rejected the name.

The elders decided for him. They gave him an immature girl, one who slept soundly at night and liked to play with younger children. "Tehmta is docile and willing," said an elder who had summoned her and placed her next to the rock. The girl looked sleepy and had an eye that looked askance and watered. She would not find a mate easily, so this was a ready choice.

Moeslet wanted to shout: "How can you give me a girl, who has no interest in fire and sleeps through storms? She won't be able to see spirits, even a flickering one." But his words would not hold much weight, and the council had spoken.

The shaman, however, sensed his objection and asked him to speak.

The Firekeeper spoke his mind. "She treats the fire as a plaything and has no sense of spirit things. How will she fight the Spirit who comes on the long nights?" There it was—he had finally spoken the secret, although he had not named it.

The elders turned to the shaman, who responded, "A Firekeeper encounters stray spirits who wander at night. But the circle of protection I cast is strong and will hold off any who would harm us."

"Is the circle strong enough to hold this spirit he speaks of?" persisted one elder, for he had some wisdom in these matters.

Taumax was not so quick to answer. "Much is not known. Sometimes a spirit can break through and stay hidden in an object which I cannot see within the circle. I will teach Moeslet a few spirit things." At that, the elders let it go.

Moeslet wanted to cry out: "That spirit can bring death to the kin, if it is not faced and fought! You don't even know its name, the one who could crush us!" He thought for a moment to say the name, so they would feel its power and realize the enormity of what a Firekeeper faced. Yet Moeslet did not speak it, for the fire had warned, "Do not give away the spirit's name, lest you lose your power."

"You're still here?" asked Taumax after the elders had left. His apprentice was to the side, ungreeted. "Are you willing to teach her?"

Moeslet did not answer.

"Remember, it is not you who decides, but the fire."

Taumax was right. He will ask the fire about her. Moeslet nodded and left.

Tehmta was eager to follow him, as she had been much neglected. Like him, she had no parents since she was small. She was excited about having a new brother or father. Still, Tehmta sensed she was not wanted and cried.

Moeslet pitied her and said, "I will teach you at the fire's bidding."

Tehmta brought the few things she had and slept near the fire. That night, Moeslet tried to keep her awake, but prod as he might past the first hour of sleep, she would just stir with her eyes shut. *This will be long and hard,* thought Moeslet. *It is well that she sleeps tonight though, for I will ask the fire about her.*

Fire did not respond that night, and Moeslet sensed it was not happy. There could be many reasons for this: any change might disturb the fire, and wouldn't it object to a young Keeper who paid little attention to it?

The next night, Fire spoke. "Why put me in the hands of someone who does not care to watch me? Tell her to go away." The fire hissed, sending jets of flame her way.

Moeslet got the response he expected, but wondered what he could do. The Council rarely changed its mind. And he couldn't just tell them what the fire had said, for they did not know of such things. He could inform the shaman and ask for advice, but it was not his decision.

Moeslet questioned the fire further. "Why do you want Tehmta to leave, when you have not tested her?"

The fire cackled harshly. "Do you think I cannot see? She is a slow, half-eyed one! I am tired of humans. I will leave on my own."

A threat like this was serious, and Moeslet became fearful. Even if the fire was not planning to expire, it could become wild and spread around them, or suddenly go out.

Moeslet used his own words to answer. He had that closeness to Fire. "You talk as if I am dead. I can use someone to be with me and help me, and would you deny me that? Are you not safer with two Keepers? Give her time and see if she can learn your ways. If she cannot, I will ask for another." Moeslet was careful to speak the truth, even though it was not all the truth.

There were a few moments before the fire consented. "Do as you say."

The quickness of the fire's decision surprised Moeslet. But the relief he felt quickly disappeared, for the fire added, "If she is not worthy, I will take her."

Moeslet sighed. It was a terrible burden. For if she failed, the fire would keep its word. It had happened before. There was another who had not fed the fire properly, nor kept its rituals. And the fire had taken a life with its flames.

"She may not be able to change," Moeslet wanted to say, but there was no going back on Fire's words. Instead, he said, "I will teach her and you will help. *The fire is the real teacher.*"

Fire did not respond, and Moeslet knew not to press any further. Perhaps he had asked too much. At least, the fire had not refused outright, so time was gained. How much time, Moeslet did not know.

Tehmta was sleeping, and sometimes the watery eye opened and looked at him. *There is a little hope...*

Progress was slow, for Tehmta played long and hard in the day and became tired like children do. Moeslet tried to be as a father and teach her things. But he knew only a few things of the day, and things that interested him did not seem to interest her. When he told her stories that hinted of larger, secret powers, she looked beyond him. She liked stories about animals, the birds of the air, or worms in the ground.

Once he told her a few secrets about the *Obtwust*, for that was not forbidden to a new Keeper. She asked why it hungered for people, as if that were nothing to ask.

Another time, he tried to tell her about the dying spirits of animals, and she said the spirits wanted colored stones and flowers. She picked up a few small stones and pulled petals from a flower, then raised them in her cupped hands.

Moeslet became angry. "Do you think dying spirits want flowers and pebbles?" Tehmta became so crestfallen that Moeslet reached out to accept her gift.

Tehmta withdrew it. "I will give these to Fire, who is always warm to me."

Moeslet was thrice surprised––her tossing the objects into the flames, calling the fire by name, and by what the fire did next. It softened.

This happened again after he called her a name, and the fire rose to her defense. "Why do you call her stupid? Do you know her thoughts?"

Moeslet's surprise gave way to laughter. It was true. He hardly knew what she was thinking. But then, he didn't care, for she did not have the thoughts of a Keeper.

Yet Moeslet saw hope in all this. The fire had taken a liking. It was the way with fire, if one spent enough time...

Moeslet learned this trick. He would mutter words against Tehmta, causing the fire to rise to her defense. Maybe Fire knew the game, for it was smart and could read many human things. Still, any talk with Fire was some type of liking. It was progress, but he realized that this liking by fire would not keep her alive if she did not perform the duties of a Keeper.

There was hope, but Moeslet did not place his hopes too high. The fire had not yet spoken directly to her. She would still have to prove herself. This was like Fire, friendly and warm enough to all, but hard to truly know.

Days passed and progress was slow. Tehmta could now stay awake halfway through the night and sometimes longer. But she never stayed awake long enough to greet the dawn. Even worse, she showed no sign of hearing the fire's words.

There was one small thing which hinted she might yet succeed. Sometimes, she woke at the coldest hour of night and looked dreamily at the fire for a time. It was no mood that spoke of being able to fight the Spirit of the Long Night, but at least she woke at the right time.

Moeslet tried to shrug off the thought he was failing. In time, Tehmta would learn to tend the fire, but she showed no sign of being strong enough to face the Obtwust. What could be done? How could he explain this to the Council?

The short days of winter came, and the time of the long night approached. Moeslet worked hard to have Tehmta stay awake a full night. But a moment's inattention in the hour before dawn, and she was asleep. Why did he try so hard? he wondered. She could not help him, anyway.

Nothing happened on the longest night itself, but the *Obtwust* came two nights later. Perhaps it had visited elsewhere and would not desire to take again.

The spirit was in a mood that Moeslet could not describe. It noted the new Keeper who was sleeping. The *Obtwust* spoke to her as if she could hear.

"Child of the Slanted Eye, will you be the new Keeper, the one who will wrestle me?"

To Moeslet's amazement, Tehmta spoke with her eyes closed. "Are you the funny beast that likes to hide in the dark? I wonder if you are hungry tonight."

Moeslet cringed, unable to bear her answer. To use her own words *and* to talk about the Obtwust's hunger was the worst possible thing. Moeslet had felt its stark hunger at the darkest time. He dared not address that, for its hunger alone could kill.

Moeslet knew better than to interfere, however, once she had loosed her words. He had not yet thought to teach her about how to talk to the spirit. Still, the *Obtwust* was talking to her, and that was better than stony silence. The spirit was in a mood, and the *Obtwust* did not seem to mind her answer.

It even spoke without Moeslet hearing, and the girl mouthed back words he couldn't make out. Then the *Obtwust* left without a fight.

Moeslet could not believe this. What had been spoken? Why did the *Obtwust* leave without battle? It was unexplained, but the *Obtwust* was its own being, and one could not predict its ways. It was luck, Moeslet decided. The Half-eye must have said something that amused the spirit and had been satisfied.

Still, Moeslet was left uneasy, more than if he had fought the *Obtwust*. For the spirit had not shown its dangerous side to Tehmta, and she was not aware of the danger. To be liked by the *Obtwust*, if this was like, was surely dangerous. For he knew that this spirit could change in an instant and with its force crush her and the kin.

He tried to explain the next day. "You must be careful. The spirit you spoke to has the power of death."

"It won't hurt me," Tehmta asserted. "I will give it flowers and pebbles."

Moeslet angered. "You are hopeless! A flower and a stone may work with Fire, but it will not work with this spirit. It is much more than fire. It will take much more to appease it. You must learn how to *fight* this Spirit when it comes, or the kin will die."

Tehmta was distracted by a bright yellow bird pecking at the ground. Moeslet tossed a stone at the bird and left Tehmta crying.

How could the elders give me this slanted-eye girl who thinks all she meets can be easily pleased? And she, who doesn't even play with fire, would play with the Obtwust! She barely knows that fire can kill. There is only one way this can end. She will end up dying, and I will have to train another. I must tell the shaman today.

Moeslet revealed his fears to Taumax, but he was not alarmed. "If she can talk to night spirits without fear, does this not show promise? Does she not have some power?"

Moeslet came dangerously close to revealing more. "She knows not to whom she talks!"

The shaman saw Moeslet was withholding, but indulged, "If this spirit, whatever it is named, left at the playful words of this girl, do we really need to fear it?"

Moeslet almost shouted, *"You do not know; the Obtwust will just as likely kill her the next time it comes."*

"What is it then?" asked Taumax.

Moeslet kept his silence.

The shaman shrugged. "No matter. Tehmta can be taught to fight a spirit in time. She loves life, does she not? She will fight, even if it be against the Spirit of Death."

Moeslet stared at Taumax, wondering if he knew more than he said. No, it was just a manner of speaking. Still, the shaman was right. Tehmta must learn to fight, and the fire would have to help him.

That night, Moeslet took the matter to Fire. "You defend Tehmta, but will you help her learn the Keeper's ways? I have talked to the shaman. I will try to teach her how to battle the Spirit of the Long Night, but this one-eyed girl is slow."

As expected, the fire rose to her defense. "I will teach her, but first she must be burned."

It was the risk of asking Fire to do anything, the price it might exact.

Moeslet felt protective and wanted to say, *"Don't burn her. She is only a child."* But the fire was right. Only when she experienced the danger of fire, would she learn.

"Promise not to hurt her badly," was all Moeslet could say.

The fire did not answer. A being without flesh and blood did not know pain, although it could hear spirits cry.

"This girl child is still young and weak," Moeslet persisted. "She is used to only minor pains."

The fire considered, and its answer showed some liking. "I will not burn her lightly, nor will I burn her badly."

CHAPTER SIX
THE TRIAL OF FIRE

THE SPRING ANIMALS came in abundance, with large herds winding through the mountain passes. Reindeer were killed, and there was plenty of food. The women dried meat and laid it in salt for use later when water would bring the meat back to life. Sometimes Moeslet would stay up in the day to watch. Tehmta was old enough to cook, and a woman taught her. She liked to place food over the fire and came to know the fire this way.

There was a trick too that Moeslet used. He would make up things that the birds were saying as they sang at dawn. Tehmta woke just before dawn, when the birds started talking. Then he discovered she had a gift, that she knew their language.

Moeslet would say the bird is talking about its future hunt, that it would search for worms that day. Tehmta would correct him. "No, the bird is greeting its family." He would say that the birds are calling their friends, and she would say, "No, the birds are happy that the light has come." He pretended to be interested in stories about the birds and flowers she loved. Tehmta would make up silly things, for she craved attention, and he used this craving to teach her.

Still, Moeslet knew it was just a start. The fire would have to do its work. *Why is it waiting? The fire has its own time...*

One day, Leola, who had healed from her lost child, visited and asked, "Do you like her?"

Moeslet felt the faint stirring of her jealousy. *Leola still loves him. She always would.*

"I would like her more," he replied, "if she could tend the fire for a full night. Then you and I could go into the day and visit the animal's hiding place."

Leola blushed, then became angry. "You must never say things like that!" She immediately regretted it, but it was too late. Moeslet got up and left, and after that he did not answer her.

Leola tried to ease his anger later. "Moeslet, you and I—we've always talked."

Moeslet answered with a saying. "*One should stay with the one who is given.*" Moeslet's heart had hardened. There would be no more free flow of words between them, and they would both feel the loss.

It pained him so much that he would have to go to someone to help hold his heart. To whom should he go? The shaman was good for spirit things. Tehmta was too young. So he took the matter to his only other friend.

"Who is she to you?" asked Fire. "She doesn't stay up with you in the night as I do."

The fire was cold in this way. It did not know the love between a man and a woman. The fire was only one sex, and it saw sexes the same way. If one spent little time together, how could another mean very much? The fire did not know that love has a long memory and could be kept alive by embers.

Fire teased, "Tehmta stays with you, although she doesn't stay awake for long."

It was a mistake to have told Fire, Moeslet decided. But who else could he trust with this private thing? Not the *Obtwust*.

So Moeslet kept talking, as if the fire were a person. Fire heard, but it could not hear his love. Rather, the fire felt his burning anger and the cry of his lost desire, a pain that made Moeslet want to hurl himself down a cliff.

Fire felt this as a danger to itself, so it said, "I will kill Ishman."

Moeslet instantly became alarmed. "This is not a killing matter! Ishman is one of the kin. *Do not kill the kin,* is one of the first rules."

Fire did not delay its response. "*If someone threatens your life, you may kill.* When someone does this, I will burn it."

"Humans are not like fire," taught Moeslet. "*We care for you, but you are not one of us.*" If that were not saying enough, he added, "*If unbidden, a fire should not meddle in human things.*"

The fire had no real bonds with humans beyond its Keeper, and it did not mention the matter again. Moeslet thought the matter was resolved.

A full moon later, Ishman died. It happened at a hunting camp a distance away and was said to be an accident.

Moeslet's suspicions were aroused by the daughter fire. Wandering bison had stampeded through the night camp. Why hadn't the bison gone around the fire, and why hadn't the hunters awakened, gathered torches, and steered the bison away? How was it that the fire had gone weak, and the bison had only killed Ishman?

A returning hunter told him, "The fire was only glowing embers when the bison came."

The camp had taken a daughter ember from Fire, so the mother fire was part of it. If she were part of his death, it would mean that the fire would have to be killed. If the Firekeeper took the matter to the elders, there would be a trial, and they would have to decide the fire's guilt.

Moeslet was uncertain what to do. *Was it by chance that Ishman lost his life? Or had the mother fire spoken against Ishman?* Although it was sad to lose a kin, Moeslet felt happy underneath, for Leola was free to be his friend again. He would now talk to her, forgive her.

Yet this time would be short, for she would soon be with another. There were two older men who had no partner, as one of theirs had died in childbirth and another from disease.

Moeslet questioned the fire directly. "How did Ishman die? Did you play a part, as you wished before?"

Moeslet had to ask, as if the fire were guilty. It was the only way to see if the fire had gone bad.

Fire, however, was wary and kept its silence at first. It knew enough of human ways to know its life was being questioned. The silence which for humans might show guilt did not mean so for Fire. It had to be careful, for it was the nature of fire to answer truly.

Moeslet hoped the fire was innocent, for he did not want to take the matter to the Council. There were good reasons. Fire was his longest friend, and it was a strong rule not to betray a friend. Then, too, he would have to tell of his feelings for Leola, and it was his rule not to speak freely of this. Last, the elders might wonder if Moeslet himself had enlisted the fire. If they so decided, they would banish him from the kin. They might even cast him into the fire, and after his death, put the fire out. Something like that had happened long ago. Moeslet recalled a story which might hold a clue in this matter.

Long ago a Keeper had attempted a day love. As he spent more time awake in the day, the night shift became more difficult. Soon, the Keeper slept during the early morning hours. The fire sometimes discovered he and his partner sleeping near it, when it should have been tended.

The fire would be left hungry for hours, and its anger rose. One night when the woman slept apart from the man, the fire overleapt its bounds and killed the woman. The Keeper grieved sorely, but the Council had no mercy. As was their custom, each elder had two stones: one burnt dark for death and a lighter one for life. The burnt stones mounded up, and the Keeper was found guilty for causing the fire's deed. He was thrown into the fire, but it did not burn him right away, and they wondered if he was guilty. Eventually, the Keeper collapsed for want of air, and the fire burned him. After this, the kin put out the fire and started anew.

Moeslet waited a day to ask again. "Why did Ishman die? Did you play a part?"

"I did not kill Ishman," Fire replied, who had been saving its answer. The fire was like that. It would have an answer, but would not offer it until asked. "But I would not have saved him either," it added.

Moeslet knew that this was enough to take the matter to the Council. For it had revealed its desire. Moeslet wondered if he should ask more and risk the fire's truth. But he could not imagine living without Fire, his friend. Still, a kin had died, so he asked once more. "Did you tell the daughter fire to hide itself in time of danger?"

The fire flickered silently. Would it answer a truth that would extinguish itself? He knew that a fire could not change its nature, only something humans could try to do. Still, it was difficult to ask. *Be careful what you ask the fire, for there is always a price....* Maybe this time Moeslet had gone too far.

"The daughter fire did what I desired," Fire answered, "but I did not tell it what to do."

Moeslet, as judge, considered this. The daughter fire would know of the mother fire's desire, for the daughter fire had come from its being. Yet she had done this on her own. The mother fire had not said, "Leap and catch Ishman afire," or "Hide and leave Ishman exposed."

The Council would not extinguish the mother fire for this alone, but the elders would be left uneasy. They would say words here and there, and leave less bone and wood for the fire. After a hard rain, they might even let it die. "It's time to start a new fire," they would say.

Moeslet decided not to tell the Council. "I believe you are innocent," he said.

The fire did not know of innocence or guilt, but it knew that it had escaped from one of the strangest human traits—that a life might be forfeit for another.

"I owe you a life," the fire responded.

Moeslet was astonished. He had expected a price from Fire, but the fire had granted him a gift instead. He wondered how Fire could give him a life and when he might have that need. Still, it was a remarkable thing to have. Maybe he could use this life when he became old and weak and live a few years more. There was usually a price to requests from Fire, but this time it had given freely.

The next day, the shaman asked about this very matter. "When Ishman died, they say the fire was low."

Moeslet was surprised and wary, so he answered with a saying: "A daughter fire can easily hide itself when there is no Keeper."

Taumax could think of nothing else to say, as he gazed into the mother fire. A saying was held true, unless there was evidence to counter it. Yet, he sensed there was something more, for that is the way with shamans. He almost spoke, then kept silent. Taumax could see no reason for the fire to desire the death of Ishman, and he would not accuse the fire to Fire's face. For even a shaman does not needlessly risk the anger of fire.

Taumax changed the subject. "What of Tehmta's training? Can she tend the fire fully?"

"She almost stays up the entire night," Moeslet answered, relieved the question had passed. "The fire is happy enough with her. In a year's time, she can be the Keeper in cold times when the trees are bare."

The shaman did not show surprise at this slow progress, but merely nodded. *Was he still thinking the fire had played a role in Isman's death?*

Afterwards, Moeslet reviewed his words carefully and wondered if he had lied. In this way he had become like Fire and was always looking to see if what he said was true. No, it was just that things were left out. He had learned to hide things like Fire.

Moeslet was happy. His friend, the fire, was grateful too, and had given him a gift. Moeslet resolved, however, to be doubly careful not to tell the fire about any more matters between Leola and himself. For all things were connected, and Moeslet, by his own secret desire, had a hand in Ishman's death.

CHAPTER SEVEN
A MIDSUMMER DAY

MOESLET RECONCILED with Leola. She was still grieving Ishman's death, but she sought to ease her grief and liked being with her old friend. Moeslet had let go of her slight, for he pitied her and felt guilt about Ishman's death. For a while, it seemed like they had gained back their childhood days. They laughed and played, and went to the hidden place, and Leola kissed him again to show she cared.

It was the height of summer, and Moeslet did not worry about the fire. Tehmta had many skills of a Keeper now, and she could keep the fire well enough on warm nights. He could spend entire days away if he wanted.

Moeslet was the happiest he had been in a long while, and yet he knew it would not last long. Leola would soon be given to another.

"Why do things happen the way they do?" Leola asked in one of her word flows. They were at the hidden place by the rushing stream, where light danced among entwined branches and blooms. It made everything around them look green. "Why were you born a Keeper, and I born to be with one who would die?"

The spirits decide. It is as things are," Moeslet answered with half sayings pieced together.

"Things can change too," Leola said, and she kissed him.

The swoon came again, and Moeslet was carried away. The sound of the stream became louder, as if the water were flowing right next to him. He imagined he had always been with her, that he was a skilled hunter, and they had children playing by the fire.

"Yes, it is you and I, and..." said Moeslet, holding her tight.

Leola's body suddenly tensed. "No," she said, pulling away.

"What?" asked Moeslet.

Leola wondered if Moeslet had lost his senses. So she tried to return his mind. "Who would speak for you? You have no family. And how will you provide for a family if you lived in the day? Would you still be able to tend the night fire and have others bring food to feed our family?"

"I have power," Moeslet declared. "I am the fire's friend, and I battle the night spirits."

"You are not a shaman or even a shaman's helper," Leola countered. "I know the fire is your friend, and that you fight minor spirits at night. But the fire is fickle, and the spirits you battle will not speak for you."

Moeslet felt the danger. He wanted to tell her how he fought a great spirit. He wanted to scream its name. But he refrained, for how could he claim the *Obtwust* as his parent? And if he did, would it not take him? So Moeslet stayed silent.

For some days after, Moeslet and Leola did not meet. Then came the "Height of Summer" when there was a celebration, and rules were broken.

They went to their secret place, and Leola lay with him. He felt taken away by the power of woman, and he felt all his sorrows lifted for a space. But Leola was promised to another, and this time would not happen again.

That night, the fire sensed something had changed and asked a question. It surprised Moeslet that Fire was the first to break silence. A change in its Keeper was alarming, so the fire spoke. "Does this woman of the day bring trouble to you?"

Although Moeslet had resolved not to speak about Leola, the fire somehow knew. It would not do well to leave a question hanging with Fire.

All Moeslet could think to say was to echo back the fire's question and give the reason. "She has brought trouble, but she has also brought love."

The fire did not understand love, but was content with the answer. "I will protect her too," it said.

It surprised Moeslet again, this unbidden gift. Had the fire grown weak? He heard things like this could happen after long years with fire, that it could grow too close to humans and die out for a reason that no one could fathom. This time, the promise of protection was a pure gift, for nothing had been offered in exchange. True, he had given much to Fire, and maybe this was Fire's way of giving back. *The fire is changing,* Moeslet thought, and he wondered what this could mean.

As hot as summer was, it was a sign that winter would be cold. There were other signs too: a flock of birds in unusual formation, a shower of shooting stars, and a roll of bones by the shaman. All foretold a frigid winter.

Fall had come early, and the animals were few. Moeslet saw a shadow cast over things, and that it would be a time of hunger this winter. He must be ready for the coming of long winter nights and the dark spirit. There was always a price. He had taken midsummer's pleasure before winter's harshness would come.

One night, Moeslet reminded the fire. "You have promised to teach Tehmta." He hoped he might gain some help this winter, even if it be small.

"I have already trained her," Fire replied.

"What?" asked Moeslet with surprise and anger. "When did you do this?"

"Haven't you been away some nights?"

Moeslet let this sink in, and he felt both relief and worry. The fire was teaching Tehmta without him. What secrets did it teach her? How much did Fire share? Moeslet looked at Tehmta, as if seeing her for the first time. She was gazing at the fire and listening.

Moeslet suddenly felt jealous, for the fire had found a new friend. What did it mean? Was the fire preparing—did it already *want* a new Keeper? A cold winter was coming; there would be hunger, a new friend... It was adding up.

Moeslet's heart raced. The fire was preparing her for something. Would the old Keeper die this winter? No, the fire had promised him a life. If things got bad, he would use Fire's gift. Still, he wondered what the future held.

Moeslet asked the fire: "You have taught Tehmta, but you did not burn her. Won't the winter take her, if she is not tested?"

"She is my friend," Fire replied.

So it was true. While Moeslet had wandered off, the fire had become friends with Tehmta. There was always a price. Things had changed.

Moeslet, however, doubted that Tehmta had learned enough to fight the Spirit of the Long Night. He feared the *Obtwust's* coming, for he sensed that winter's harshness meant that the spirit would use its strength in a large way. He could already feel it. There was a hunger in all of nature. It would be a *Time of Turning*, when the nature of things themselves could change. In such a turning, much would die, but new things would be born. Moeslet wondered how many would die and what new life would come.

CHAPTER EIGHT
FIRE'S NEW FRIEND

IT CAME BACK TO HAUNT Moeslet. He had broken a rule, although it was not a big one to break. He had lain with Leola, who was promised to another. The shaman wondered about their renewed friendship, and maybe it led him to wonder about Ishman's passing. It was probably, the shaman decided, no more than her going back to an old childhood friend to soothe her grief.

Still, Moeslet felt guilt, and he needed to tell someone. Because of Ishman's death, he could not take the matter to an elder. Nor could he take it to Fire, for it might make more trouble. Besides, the fire had been less of a friend of late. Maybe it was the price of the gift—to offer a life and to grow apart?

That left Tehmta. She was nearly grown now and could talk about something longer if she chose. He had tested her and found she could answer seriously and not just laugh like a child at things she did not understand. So he brought the matter to her and talked about the fire, Leola, and Ishman. Her answer surprised him.

"You want to love, but there is nowhere to place it. You gave your love to Leola... she will go away. You gave it to the fire... the fire has only one Keeper."

How can she say that? He understood about Leola, but Fire? *Could the fire have already chosen Tehmta to be its new Keeper? No, it can't be! There is much she doesn't know yet, and she doesn't know how to fight the Obtwust.*

Reading Moeslet's doubt, Tehmta raised the inside of her arm and showed him a broad, ugly scar.

"You were burned!" Moeslet exclaimed. "When did the fire teach you?"

"Last full moon."

"And you did not tell me? You did not scream and wake me?"

Tehmta did not respond. She had learned a deep secret of fire, how to keep silence in pain. There was power in silence. Moeslet had this power too, for he endured aloneness, and of a love that could not be placed. But the pain had grown too great of late.

"What will become of me, if you are to be the new Keeper? And how will you deal with the *Obtwust?*"

In his confusion, Moeslet spoke its name. Maybe he should not have, but they were like one now. For, if he was still the Firekeeper, and she was the Firekeeper to be, they were one in this in-between time.

"The fire has taught me much, and I can stay awake the full night," was her answer.

So the fire was keeping her awake at night by telling her deep things. It was making *her* the new Keeper. It happened in the lives of all Keepers, but this was coming too soon. He did not even have gray in his hair.

Moeslet wondered if this was why the fire had given him a life and why it had said it would protect Leola. It was all happening too fast, so he took the matter to Fire that night.

Moeslet pleaded his case. "Why do you rush to change Keepers, and why didn't you tell me? I haven't neglected you. Haven't I saved you from judgement and death? I have always fought by your side against the *Obtwust.* Why are you leaving without telling me and before I am old?"

Moeslet was not surprised that Fire did not answer right away, and he wondered if it would have an answer this time. Still, Moeslet sensed that silence would not remain its answer. This was not a question about death, the world beyond, the *Obtwust*, or the time of the first fire. It was simply about the fire, Tehmta, and himself.

The next day, the fire answered indirectly. "I have given you a life." So the fire had no answer for its decision. The fire had given him a gift and thought this was enough.

There began an awkward period, with the two Keepers having different shifts: the early one for the apprentice and the late one for him. Things would not be the same now, for the fire would only truly confide in one Keeper.

Moeslet prepared to become even more alone. During this in-between time, they could both hear the fire, but that would soon end. There was nothing that Moeslet could do to stop the fire's choosing. Maybe he could delay it for a few days, for there was still the matter of the *Obtwust*.

Moeslet weighed this and came directly to the fire: "Why are you choosing a new Keeper before the time of the long night? Do you see something?"

The fire had a bright eye in the night, and although it could not see well in the day, its night eye could see the future. But asking about the future was a risky matter with fire. For one, it might make it more likely the future said by the fire would hurl their way. Better to leave the future uncertain, so that when the time came, it might hang by a thread to go this way or that.

Moeslet challenged the fire. "If you go to another, who will be my friend? Leola has another. Tehmta maybe...but she is so unlike me. That leaves me no one, except the *Obtwust* who shows its love by killing."

The fire was icy and did not answer.

Moeslet could only think of one more argument. "Tehmta has learned much, but she is not ready to serve on the long night by herself. The *Obtwust* will easily take her life, and it might take yours."

The fire, like humans, wanted to preserve itself. It waited to reveal its answer to just before dawn. "You will remain Keeper on the longest night. After the Obtwust passes, Tehmta will become my Keeper."

So, Moeslet thought, *the fire will keep me, only as long as it needs me!* Less than a month was left to fight the darkness of winter before gaining the spring.

In anger Moeslet cried out, "Why should I stay with you now, when you are planning to leave me? Why shouldn't I let you die now?"

Fire knew its answer. "You will keep the oath of the Firekeeper."

It was true. A Keeper was sworn not to renounce his position until the fire gave its leave. And the Keeper was promised to the fire, especially during the darkest, coldest time. The fire's answer had brought back a flood of memories. Moeslet remembered how it came that the Obtwust was fought by the Firekeeper and how he first became one.

Long ago, fires would fight alone on the longest night, for when the *Obtwust* came, it was too much for any human to face. It was a saying in fact: *All the days of the year the Keeper helps, but on the longest night, the fire battles for its own life.*

Long ago, however, a Firekeeper risked himself to save the fire on the long night, and so the saying changed. Sayings rarely changed, but deeds could sometimes do it.

Moeslet's own first time was seared within him. The Keeper before him had fallen gravely ill, and there was no one to help the fire face this test. Moeslet had no parents, nor anyone to warm him, so he kept close to the fire even when others tried to shoo him away. So, during the darkest hour, Moeslet was alone and awake in front of the fire.

The *Obtwust* appeared surprised to see Moeslet there. "Who is this child?" it asked Fire. "How can one so young be so close to you and keep its eyes open before me?"

No one saw the *Obtwust* directly. At most, one glimpsed its outline outside the fire's light. Still, Moeslet held a steady gaze, sensing the curious presence beyond.

Because he did not know to fear this, he looked toward the *Obtwust,* steady and unwavering. He was used to facing adults on his own, the skilled hunters of the kin. There was something stubborn within him, too.

The *Obtwust* wondered at this small human, so powerless and unfearing. It would have taken the slightest gesture to extinguish him, but the *Obtwust* did otherwise. It passed him over.

"Yes, it is just like the Spirit of the Longest Night," the Keeper had said when he heard the story. "The *Obtwust* takes whoever it wants, old or young, strong or weak, laughing or crying. But look steady and show no fear, and sometimes it just passes you by. Something else may have extinguished its desire.... I don't know what it was, for the spirit had come determined to take. I know that, since this has happened, the fire will choose you as its new Keeper."

Moeslet thought the old Keeper was making things up, but he continued, saying, "How can it be otherwise? You stayed with the fire during its darkest hour. It will want you by its side next winter. The fire has already asked about you. You will be the new Keeper, but I fear for you. The time of a Firekeeper can be short.

It had happened that way years ago. Now, it seemed, Moeslet's time had come. But the old fire had become foolish. It had chosen a new Keeper before she had proved herself. At least, it allowed Moeslet to be there for this last battle. Should he stay? The thought came to him that the fire's choice could be undone. The *Obtwust* could take her, and then the fire would have no choice but to go back to him.

But Moeslet did not want to be like the *Obtwust* and decide who should leave this world or stay. He became confused and fearful, trying to see the future and its paths, none of which looked good. The winter would be bad, with hunger and death. The fire had its own plans, and there was something more, he sensed—something the fire did not share.

CHAPTER NINE
THE FIRE'S QUESTION

MOESLET MADE A HARD choice. The fire had already decided to leave him for the new Keeper. Tehmta was now tending the late hours, for the fire had chosen this too.

The fire must have its reasons. Maybe it sensed there was danger for him to stay much longer. Maybe it foresaw something and wanted her to be ready for the longest night. Had she not spoken with the *Obtwust* like it was not to be feared, something simple and easily pleased? It was foolish for her to think this, of course, but the *Obtwust* had not taken her. *The fire is the servant, but the fire approves the new Keeper.*

The kin would depend on her and the fire more than they realized, to bring warmth in the winter, to keep predators away, to cook food, and to protect the weak during sickness and birthing.

"The time is coming when you will take all the dark hours," Moeslet told Tehmta, "so I must teach you all that I know."

Tehmta looked at him steadily. She had grown; the fire had taught her much already. Moeslet went over some smaller things at first. Tehmta kept silent and listened, not saying whether she knew or not. Still, Moeslet sensed it was good to say them again, for the fire was not human, and there would be things the fire would just let happen for a harsh lesson. *The fire teaches, and the Keeper repeats.*

"Remember, the fire has its weaknesses. It is loyal, but not with a human love. If you only listen to Fire and become too alone with it, you will grow cold. You could favor the fire more than your own kind."

Moeslet searched her eyes and wondered if this was a danger. He knew that every new Keeper faced that. There were also weaknesses the fire would expose, for the fire exposed all in time.

Tehmta's bad eye had become less glazed, less droopy. Was the fire healing her? Had staring into its embers helped to dry the water?

Moeslet suddenly became afraid of the change. Why had the fire chosen her so soon? It wasn't because she could care for the fire better, or because she could defend against the dark spirit... *Had she gone over to the fire?*

Moeslet reflected that she had shown no interest in boys, and other than a few stories about birds, she talked only about the fire, its shapes and stories it told at night. It seemed she didn't mind the fire's ash on her face, and her hands often held a stick with a burning orange end.

Moeslet warned her with sayings. "*The fire is not human and has its own ways. The Keeper serves the fire, but the fire remains our servant.*"

Tehmta listened, but Moeslet wasn't sure she understood. He could hardly bear to ask her, "You have grown close to the fire. Are you thinking of going the way of fire?"

Tehmta smiled; her eyes glistened. The silence told much. Was she already bonded? It had happened before. The fire and a human had grown too close, thinking they could be one, that they could marry.

Maybe, since the death of Ishman, the fire had gone bad, breaking rules. If the Council found this out, they would surely extinguish it. But the long night was almost upon them, and Moeslet could not risk extinguishing even a bad fire.

"*You must serve the kin first,*" Moeslet said with urgency. "This rule underlies all the others."

"I will care for the kin," Tehmta responded. "But sometimes the fire and I are one."

Moeslet felt both relief and alarm. Tehmta had spoken with honesty, but there was danger in her last words. Not having another human close to her, she had grown too close to the fire. He had failed her in this, for he had held himself apart from her. Had he forgotten how small he once was until the fire lifted him up?

The following night, Moeslet revealed, "You must know about the long night. You must learn how to fight the powerful night spirit which appears then. It's named the *Obtwust*. You must try to stop it from taking the lives of the kin. Or if it must take, let it only be one."

Tehmta shrugged, not seeming to be concerned about the danger. "I have already spoken to the *Obtwust*."

Moeslet hid his surprise and dared not ask anymore. More talking about the spirit was too early. Tehmta yawned. It was almost time for the day, and she did not care to hear any more, either. "Another time," sighed Moeslet, and he turned to the fire.

THE COLD WAS COMING. Moeslet decided he would question the fire to discover its intentions. As expected, the fire did not answer right away, but while Tehmta slept, the fire spoke what seemed like parting words. Moeslet couldn't help wondering, *Could this winter be the time of a large ending and beginning?*

Moeslet started a question. "Tehmta thinks she can become one with you. But she is flesh and blood and not fire! You know the saying for when humans come into the world. *Let fire be near when you are born, but do not become one with fire, until the day you leave the world.* What do you say to this?"

The question was one whose answer could risk the fire being extinguished. Wavering and jumping with many points, the fire leapt as if reaching—one almost touched Moeslet. Although the fire seemed trapped, it told the truth, "Can I not love too?"

The fire's answer so surprised Moeslet that he wondered if all the rules of the world were breaking. This was too new, and Moeslet wondered what it could mean. The fire could not possibly know.

"You are not a human and cannot love as a human," Moeslet corrected. "You can only love as fire can. The word love can only mean what it means to a fire, unless you could become human."

The fire was not long in saying, "Then I will become human too."

Moeslet laughed. The fire had gone wild, forgetting its nature. It was a great danger for Fire to think that it was something other than what it was.

Still, the fire did not lie. So what did the words mean? Maybe it meant it could become human in some way. Maybe it could for a moment.... If Tehmta willingly joined the fire, and the fire killed her, could they not become one—before they would both go over to the Obtwust? Maybe the fire would feel human love when Tehmta's life was extinguished,

Moeslet knew something of this because he had felt the temptation before. It was early in his days as Keeper when Fire had drawn close to him. For long hours, he had felt the fire strongly as he struggled to stay awake during the darkest part of the night. Moments came in which he seemed to be one with Fire, so much so that he could walk through it without being hurt.

One night, Fire asked him to *stay* in the fire, but he refused. The end of Fire's desire was to be extinguished by fire. Could it be any other way? How else could you become one with Fire?

"*You cannot make new rules by words alone,*" Moeslet had answered.

The fire leapt as if to engulf him, but Moeslet had taken the precaution to stand a distance away. He had not forgotten. No matter how close you came to Fire, it had a side that could bring you death.

Later, Moeslet decided on another approach to correct Fire, one that would risk the fire's anger. He let the fire's fuel go low.

"Feed me more," the fire demanded.

Moeslet did not move. "Have you forgotten you are a servant to humans, that you do not rule us?"

Fire's anger rose with crackling and flashes of red. "Will you starve me until I agree with you?"

"You are not human; is that not obvious enough?" asked Moeslet. "You are fed dried bones and wood, not flesh and green plants. You do not drink water, for that would kill you. Likewise, you cannot love as humans do. You do not beget children who differ from you, but only a fire exactly like you.

"Still, the kin need you. Fire gives us light, warmth, and hope in the darkness when our thoughts go deep. You love in a way, but not with a human love."

The fire did not understand. It thought it could know all things, cast its light everywhere and see, and that it was enough.

Moeslet let the fire go to red embers until it begged. It was harsh and cruel, but he had to teach Fire. It must not be allowed to forget its nature. For the fire's hope to love a human could lead it to engulf and kill that human. Although Tehmta might not believe him, he would warn her of the danger, that there was a darkness in the fire's love.

CHAPTER TEN
THE WINTER COUNCIL

THE COUNCIL WAS DUE to meet before winter's coming. Moeslet would bring the matter of the new Keeper to them. He would be careful, though, not to raise questions about the fire.

There was also a matter, he sensed, something much greater than him. Something major would happen this winter, more than a single year's turning. It would be a *Great Turning*, such that the world would never be the same. Moeslet did not know what this change might be.

The Council met several times during the year, but only before winter did the Firekeeper come. They would bring him in, not to hear his wisdom, or to ask what he thought on some important matter. They would ask: "Can you keep the fire bright through the dark winter? Will you wake us if you need help, even if it be on the longest night?"

Among ancient roots of an oak, mirrored by gnarled branches above, the Council met. The bark of the exposed roots had been chewed as food, and the ground about them had been scoured for bits of tinder.

It surprised the Council when Moeslet brought Tehmta, who needed to hear their words too. There was much to worry about. The weather had turned early, and animals were scarce. Everyone knew there would be hunger, and the group was at risk. The kin had survived before, but there was a feeling this winter might be different.

Leola's new partner, an older man named Tiquan, had come to the meeting. She was already with child, and Moeslet had not seen her much of late. There was no mention of him being the Firekeeper for this child's birthing.

Moeslet still remembered the night of the stillbirth, when the midwives held up the silent baby and laid him in the fire. It seemed for a moment that the fire did not burn the child. One rarely gave a human to a fire, lest it change the fire's nature. But the daughter fire was to be extinguished, and after the child and it were cinders, the fire would know no more of its deed.

The eldest of the Council began, "We know that winter's cold has come early, and the time of hunger will be long. We need to prepare." He looked toward the shaman, who spoke next.

"It is so. There will be attacks from animals and humans. We must not let the winter make us weak."

"The kin will survive," declared another. "Someone will die and provide food. It has happened this way before."

"Maybe, maybe not," said Tiquan. "But why should we leave this matter to chance? Should we wait until we become weak? Why wait for wolves to attack us? Won't the hunger of the human hunters be great as well?"

"We will fight them off like before," said the shaman.

Many spoke at once, asking questions: "What if we are too weak to fight? What if too many come? What will we do?"

"I propose another way," announced Tiquan.

"We will not take lives like the others," guessed the shaman.

"Let me speak. We will not take an unwilling life. We will cast bones, and the bones will decide. In that way we will show courage by being willing to die."

The shaman did not approve. "You have heard the saying, *It is not for the kin to choose who lives or dies.* The rule has held us well for long. If we start to decide this one or that one dies, have we not opened a new way for death to come?"

Tiquan did not give up. "At least we will be alive to face death's next coming. Is not the oldest saying: *Live! Do what is necessary to live!*"

Taumax did not come back with the saying: *Life is given, and life should not be taken.* Many on the Council, he could tell, agreed with Tiquan because they had young children who were at risk.

So it was agreed. If the kin were near death, and there was no other way, they would do this other thing.

Moeslet did not like this, but at least he was in the circle. Or so he thought, until an elder added, "Only the hunters will cast bones, for the choice must be among those who have been tested and shown courage."

It stung Moeslet, but he did not have time for self-pity. He was ordered by an elder, "Speak of the fire and its strength this winter."

Moeslet looked the elder in the eye. "The fire will remain alive, but there will be a change of Keepers."

His response caused surprise and alarm, for there was always a danger during a change in Keepers.

"Can it not wait?" asked Taumax.

"The fire has chosen another."

There must have been something in Moeslet's voice, for some of the Council laughed anxiously.

"What of the time around the longest night?" asked the shaman.

"She will become the Keeper after then," said Moeslet.

This seemed to satisfy Taumax, but he still sensed something was wrong. He asked a shaman question, which revealed that he knew more. "Why has the fire chosen so early? Has the fire been a loyal servant?"

Moeslet paused, for he knew this was a testing question, and the fire's fate hung on his words. What could he say that would not reveal his doubts? He had taken on the fire's trait of telling the truth, but how could he betray a friend? And it would be at the worst time.

All eyes were upon him, and some sensed his hesitation might mean that there was trouble with the fire.

Moeslet, who was sometimes slow in answering, said, "Tehmta is ready to serve the fire, and the fire is ready to serve Tehmta. I sense there is a special danger this winter, but we are prepared. As for our hunger, I think we should keep to the ways of old."

The last part of his answer did what Moeslet wanted. All in the Council jumped on this, not noticing that Moeslet should have said, *Tehmta is ready to serve the fire, and the fire is ready to serve the kin.*

Angrily, the elders asked, "How can you question the Council's decision? You should stay to the things of the fire."

Still, the shaman had not missed this change of speech, and afterwards, he brought the matter to Moeslet.

"You say the fire and Tehmta serve one another? Is there not a danger in this?"

"Tehmta still serves the kin, and the fire will keep its bounds."

Taumax nodded, not quite satisfied. He knew that, early in a firekeeper's journey, the fire might become specially bonded with its new Keeper, but that this should quickly pass. And this was happening at a critical time.

Taumax said no more. If he was going to challenge Moeslet, he would have done so at the Council. The shaman decided it was best not to risk upsetting things, for the winter would be perilous enough.

The shaman added one thing. "A young Firekeeper who makes a mistake will not likely survive the winter. Do not hand over your power until you are sure."

It was the last thing the old Firekeeper would do, to choose the exact time when Keepers changed, although he could not delay the matter for long.

"The kin will survive," Moeslet answered.

The shaman looked deep into Moeslet's eyes and saw that he spoke true. He sighed, knowing how much relied on this small one, more than the others would know. "You are brave," said Taumax. "I know you fight more than sleep, darkness, and cold on the Long Night."

Moeslet hid his surprise. How much did the shaman know, and for how long? He looked back at the times when he had fought the *Obtwust*, when another shape as a great black cat had appeared. Had not the night cat saved him at the critical times? The shaman said nothing all these years. So why was he saying things now?

"I didn't know," was all Moeslet could think to say.

The shaman hardly seemed to listen. He was searching within himself. "It will be a winter of peril," he said. "We must speak again."

The first raid came early, when the hunger was just starting. The kin were surprised when the worst Hunters of Humans came, those who brandished heads on staffs. They descended from the mountains during the day, an unexpected time while Moeslet slept. When he woke, the battle was ending with signs of confusion around him. A kin had been killed and dragged away.

Moeslet looked about, alarmed. All seemed to be present––Leola, the hunters, the women, and children. All the families were safe.

Then he realized that the worst had happened. The shaman, the person on whom all the kin relied, was gone.

How could the Fearsome Ones have succeeded in this? It could not be just the lucky flight of a spear. It could only be by deep shamanic power and surprise.

Taumax had two apprentices: a boy who was too young to have learned but basic things, and an older girl, not yet trained enough to take his responsibilities. She was gifted, but did not yet know of deeper things. She had told him, "Taumax said you were brave to face the night alone."

Moeslet gathered she knew little more than this. And even if she had heard about the *Obtwust,* she wouldn't be much help. Moeslet saw the worst of winter was fast approaching, like a black cloud that would swallow the sun.

He wondered if the fire had known that the shaman would die. Did the fire somehow know that the winter would be especially perilous, that the kin would not stop the Spirit of the Long Night from claiming its share?

Late that night, Moeslet risked asking the fire about the future. "The winter does not look good. The Spirit of the Long Night will be hungry. Will the kin survive?"

He should not have asked, he suddenly sensed, but he could not take the question back.

"I do not know if the kin will survive, " answered Fire. 'But a Keeper will die."

CHAPTER ELEVEN
PREPARATIONS

THE LONG NIGHT WAS a moon away, but Moeslet did not know how to prepare Tehmta with so little time. And what good was preparation? The fire had said one would die. Yes, the fire could see the future, but still it may not be so. It might mean that one Keeper would leave the fire. It would have been better not to have asked, for enough had already happened. The shaman had died, and the fire was turning toward Tehmta.

True, the new Keeper could stay up through the longest part of the night, but that was just facing the night and cold. What of the *Obtwust*? Tehmta would need him, as Moeslet had unknowingly relied on the shaman. But he was no shaman, and Taumax had only shown him a few things. Maybe his spirit was still present, although Moeslet did not sense it. He was on his own—except *for Fire, who had promised him a life. But what good is a life, if the rest of the kin were to die?*

Moeslet saw that Tehmta sensed the urgency of things. Maybe the fire had taught her about the true danger of the *Obtwust*. Maybe the fire had told her secret things, just to draw her close.

Moeslet decided that no matter what she had been taught, they must talk about the dark spirit. He was not sure what he could teach her, for the spirit was too unpredictable to say "do this" or "do that." Still, he must tell her what he knew.

Moeslet started that night. "The time of deep winter is coming. It is the test of every Keeper. This night is not just about facing the dark and cold. There are night spirits, and a powerful, dark spirit who takes lives to appease its great hunger." Moeslet did not name the spirit, for to do so was to half-summon it.

"Yes, we have spoken of this spirit before and named it," said Tehmta, who knew that names were powerful.

Moeslet worried that her tone was too casual. "Who knows its real name? It is likely one of many."

"Where does its power come from?" asked Tehmta, trying to find another name.

Moeslet didn't know. It was a good question, for all power comes from somewhere. Who could penetrate this secret of the *Obtwust*? "Maybe the fire knows," he finally answered. "We will ask for the fire to help us too."

Tehmta had the sense to ask, "You have faced this spirit before. How have you defeated the *Obtwust*?"

Something stirred in the wind, and Moeslet warned, "Do not use its name unless you must! One thing I know—do not act fearful. Stay awake and face it. Be strong! The spirit will test you, and it may or may not pass over you."

"I have faced it before."

"Then you should know it is not a plaything. It ends things; it takes lives! And it will take you, like any other."

Tehmta showed doubt for the first time. She wanted to be the Keeper and had not resisted the fire's advances. But she was not fully prepared for this.

"Is this not a matter for shamans?" she asked.

Moeslet remained silent. He could not speak of the danger in which the shaman's dying had placed them.

Tehmta read his face and became frightened. "Will I live? I do not want to become the Keeper to die!"

"The fire has decided, and you have accepted. You must not go back on this, for we need you and the fire's help."

"So Fire will know what to do?"

Moeslet hesitated. "The fire has stayed by my side during the time of testing. It did not go out, and I gained strength from it."

Moeslet would ask the fire for special help this winter. He wondered how he would ask so that Fire would respond right away.

It became colder, the days shorter, and the kin's hunger grew. There were two more attacks, but they were from stragglers, and the kin drove them back. The ones who took the shaman had not returned. Maybe they still wrestled with his spirit.

Because the fire might be right about the death of a Keeper, Moeslet visited Leola more often. She was showing more, but the midwives had said that her time was not yet. That was good, for she must birth after the long night. It had happened before, that she had birthed too close to this time. Maybe that was why he had been chosen to fight the *Obtwust,* and why his body was handicapped, the imprint of a battle with invisible forces.

Moeslet recalled the story of his own birthing, when his mother had died from loss of blood. "Did you know that you almost died, too?" asked the midwife. "The cord was wrapped around your neck, and your body was blue. Your mother, although weak from blood loss, shook you and cried, 'Begone spirit! Do not take my child! Take me!'"

"How could a mother order the dark spirit?" Moeslet had asked. The question was one for a shaman to answer, but a midwife was like his equal—for if the shaman can heal persons close to death, a midwife brought new lives into the world. "There is a spirit that takes lives at its whim," she had answered. "She fought this spirit and won."

"My mother died!" Moeslet objected.

"She won your life," returned the midwife. "A mother's life is usually saved over a newborn, but a mother may offer her life in its place."

Moeslet wondered at the enormity of this and why his mother had given so much. "But my mother did not know me," he said.

"She did," said the midwife. "She felt you inside; she listened to your silent words."

Moeslet did not know what to say to this, and the midwife went on, "When such ones are saved, they have a special reason for being in the world."

Yes, thought Moeslet, *a gift—of all gifts to have — to fight the Obtwust. But what good is that, when it only brings me danger?*

His mind returned to the present. The kin were imperiled by hunger, cold, and the coming of the dark spirit. He did not know if he could hold off the *Obtwust* this time. He had thought before that he could. He had even thought he could teach another. But the shaman was gone and had died before he could complete his teaching with Moeslet. There were rituals, signs, and words of power that Moeslet did not know. He only knew one warding off sign: his hands crossed over his chest. But he did not know what word went with the sign.

Much bore down upon Moeslet, and he spoke to Leola. "Life has gone on, and I have watched it pass. You have chosen another."

"He was chosen for me," Leola defended. Her eyes still showed that she loved him.

The pain rose in Moeslet. He would have to win this battle, if only for her and her child.

"What is it?" she asked.

Moeslet kept his pain silent. For a moment he remembered his joy during the midsummer day, and his pain abated. He left her with a faint smile, wondering if this was the last time.

The night sky held a quarter moon, and the lengthening nights ate away at the day. The kin's hunger became stronger, and there was talk of casting bones. They would need to do it soon.

Moeslet took his question to Fire. It answered, but not in the way he had hoped. "The *Obtwust* can be fought, but it cannot be defeated."

"We must do what we can. Teach us how to fight it," Moeslet demanded.

The fire did not answer.

"You know, but you will not tell!" Moeslet challenged. "Do you want the kin to die? Who is this *Obtwust* that you will not teach us? Does it bring you food? Does it fan you so you can blaze? Does it stay with you during the long nights, or does it come and go when it pleases."

It was true the *Obtwust* came at other seasons. Its mood was different then, such that one might not know that it was the same spirit. It was like the weather—breezy and new when spring came, warm and mild in the summer. But Moeslet did not forget the spirit held the power of the long night, and it was best to avoid it, even on those pleasant summer days.

The fire did not answer, and the next time it talked of other things. There was nothing Moeslet could do, but he gained a clue. The fire knew more, but was not ready to tell.

"Maybe you can find out more from the fire," Moeslet asked Tehmta. "It must touch upon one of the fire's deep secrets. Be careful. Do not promise the fire too much."

Tehmta asked for two nights, but the fire did not answer her.

"What are we to do?" Moeslet asked Tehmta, not expecting her to answer.

"Somehow, we must use this spirit's strength against itself," she replied.

Moeslet laughed. "You do not know the *Obtwust*. It has but one mind when it comes to kill."

The days were running out, and Moeslet was left to this last idea. "There is another way to gain answers. We can use the fire to summon the shaman's spirit. We must be careful, for the spirits of the dead, even those of friends, can be perilous."

The summoning should have been guided by a shaman, and Moeslet had asked the shaman's apprentice for help. *"It is best to leave the dead alone,"* she had said. It was only a saying and did not consider what sometimes needed to be done.

So, he would do it himself. Other than Fire, the shaman had been the closest he had to a father.

The summoning came, and it was brief. The fire crackled colors, and the shaman's spirit rode the flame.

"How do we stop the *Obtwust*?" Moeslet asked directly. "How do we preserve the kin?"

A distant voice spoke out of the fire. "The time of taking is at hand, and this spirit will not be denied. A great change is coming."

"Tell us what to do, so at least some of the kin survive!"

"You will know when the time comes," said the shaman, his voice fading into the fire.

The message was mostly disturbing. They had gained no special knowledge, but were only assured that it would come later.

Moeslet tried to hold on to this hope. Maybe there was a way to keep the *Obtwust* from taking all. But the hope was *thin,* and the coming of the New Year hung by a thread.

Two days later a scout reported that the Fearsome Ones who had killed the shaman were near, and the thread became thinner. Moeslet realized they should expect another attack. For if they could take their shaman, would they not come back for more as the winter progressed? The kin would be weaker, without a shaman, and surely they could kill one or two. Could Moeslet blame them? Were they not following the first rule: *Live and do what is necessary to live*?

The kin no longer talked of tossing bones, for they knew there would be battle and there would be dead. The shaman was right: a large change was coming. Would the kin be no more?

CHAPTER TWELVE
THE LONGEST NIGHT

THE DAY BEFORE THE long night, the sky was cloudless and brilliant blue. It was bitter cold. The kin huddled in the cave's mouth around the blazing fire. They had gathered all the wood and old bones from kills they could find. The Keepers had lain down to sleep during the day. There was hunger, but there was more fear than hunger.

"Do you know what we will do?" Tehmta had asked before falling asleep.

Moeslet had hid his uncertainty. "We will know when the time comes. It is best not to worry. The spirit will likely put you into a deep sleep. It has the power to cast such a spell."

"Why would it do this?"

"One cannot predict its ways. And another thing: this spirit does not usually take right away, but it likes to wrestle first. I do not understand, for no fight is fair with it. The spirit will test before it takes. But it may not take. Once on a long night, when I was sick and could barely stay awake, the shaman stayed by my side. I could sense the *Obtwust's* power was strong. A gesture and I would be sent to death. But it did not do so. Instead, it put me into a deep sleep.

"Afterwards, I saw the shaman, tired and worn. When I asked him what had happened, he said, 'The night was cold and long. It was hard to keep the fire lit.' I had believed that the dark spirit had come and passed us over. Now I know Taumax had *wrestled* the *Obtwust* without me."

"I will not be put to sleep! I will stay awake and fight."

Moeslet knew this was the talk of someone who did not know the *spirit's* power.

"Sleep now," said Moeslet, "for the time to sleep is short."

When Moeslet and Tehmta woke once during the day, the fire was strong, and preparations were being made for defense. A spy of the Human Hunters had been spotted. The men sharpened and hardened their spears and the women piled stones to throw.

Except for two watchmen, the band of kin went to their sleeping spaces deeper within the cave. The longest night had begun, and for much of it, there was no sign of danger. Moeslet and Tehmta gazed upon the fire and one another, and it seemed like no spirit would break the night's calm.

Something shifted. A bitter cold descended and pressed against them like death. Just as the force felt like it would be too much, the *Obtwust* came, falling like a heavy blanket around them.

Moeslet did not flinch, but steeled himself. Tehmta, amazed and frightened, resolved to keep her eyes open, even as it drained her.

There was the first moment of decision; what would the *Obtwust* do? Would it leave like the wind or take lives in a single fury? Or would it stay to test before deciding? It was usually wrestling it sought, and this time was no different.

Moeslet's plan had been to let the *Obtwust* make the first words. To his surprise, Tehmta spoke. "Why do you come at night to harm us? The kin are a few people, cold and hungry. Are there not others you could take, like the ones who kill humans? They would be more of a fight than us, two small Firekeepers."

A big mistake! thought Moeslet, wondering at the many words Tehmta had loosed. Too late, he had forgotten to tell her. It was not good to challenge the *Obtwust* right after its coming. Nor was it good to admit weakness. Still the words had been said, and Moeslet had to stand by them. He added, "We may be small and weak, but we will stand and fight to preserve the kin."

The *Obtwust* did not like to hear pleas before fighting. It wanted strength to be met by strength.

"Why does this powerful spirit trifle with us?" Moeslet had once asked.

"Spirits have their ways," the shaman had answered.

"Can a spirit change its ways?"

"You ask shaman questions," Taumax observed, but he did not answer.

The darkness shifted, and the *Obtwust* spoke. "If you are weak, why have you been chosen to face me on the long night? Are there not others, stronger among you? Where are they? You must have special powers. Why else would the kin with all its great hunters depend upon you?"

Moeslet defended the kin the best he could. "The hunters have their duty. They protect us from the animals of the night and the ones who hunt heads."

"So they do," the *Obtwust* agreed.

It was a good sign that the spirit had engaged them. It did not just act. But Moeslet was worried, for when it came time to act, there would be no shaman to help him.

The voice of Taumax had said as much, that it would take this night but would not take all. *For the power of the Obtwust is given in its words, and it will not go back on them. So take the words...* Moeslet had heard this saying from somewhere. But where? Had it been from the shaman or the fire?

Moeslet must say more, but he couldn't find any words. Every word with the *Obtwust* was crucial. He wished that Leola was there to help him. Tehmta's gaze was steady, but she said nothing. There was deathly silence, and the dark spirit waited.

"We must say something," Moeslet whispered.

Tehmta was frightened, for she sensed death was close.

"Speak!" pleaded Moeslet. "Anything!"

Tehmta half-stuttered: "We may be weak, but we can do many things. We keep the fire awake, which warms us and cooks our food. We tell children stories in the evening. We have waved branches of fire to keep the hungry animals away. And we face you."

"So you do," said the Obtwust, who seemed to like her response. "Tell me, what else do you do?"

Tehmta had said all she could think, but this time, Moeslet found some words. "We know the spirit of fire, and we talk to Fire. We know the spirit of new life, and we help keep new life alive. We know the spirit of animals, and we offer them back to the Mother of Animals. But we do not know you, or why you come to take us! We know you have great power. And we know we must fight you. But how can we stand against you?"

Moeslet did not know if his challenge was too strong, but he knew this much: to have a chance, one must wrestle the *Obtwust.*

The dark spirit's anger rose, and it was not a pleasant thing. "Do you not know me? I come on the long night, and I come on a mild, spring day. ? Do you not sense me in the storm with its lightning and thunder? Do you not know me in the falling rain and the rainbow that follows? I know the fierce leopard and the singing bird. I know the fierceness of fire and the calming of water. I am there at death and new life. And you say you do not know me?"

"We know that you put out lives and take away our babies! Why do you do these things?" Moeslet challenged.

The *Obtwust's* anger wrapped like a fist around them. "I will *take* this night. I will take a Keeper, and when the Fearsome Ones come, they will take many of you! Only a few will survive."

"No!" cried Moeslet. "Let only one be taken—me! You must protect the kin from the headhunters!" It suddenly came to him that this could be the way. He would ask the *Obtwust* for help and offer his life.

The *Obtwust* laughed, if laugh it was. "Do you think your life is worth many? You are bold, Firekeeper. I will take Tehmta and many others and leave you for another time."

"No! The fire has chosen Tehmta as its new Keeper. The kin need her."

The *Obtwust* paused ever so slightly, as if Moeslet's words held some power. Still, it remained obdurate. "Would you tell me *who* to take? Can you stop me? I will put you in a deep slumber, and you will not even remember what happened. I will take a Keeper and leave one behind, as I have said."

It was more words. It was more power given to them, to learn about the *Obtwust* and its intentions. But the words were not good. And what had they learned? The *Obtwust* had spoken as if its words could not be undone, as if its words bound itself.

Moeslet looked at Tehmta. Her face had fallen and was streaked with tears. Still, he was amazed that she did not whine or plead for her life.

Then another voice spoke, surprising all. It was Fire. "Do not take my Keeper, for she and I are one. If you must, take me and not her!" Moeslet could not believe the fire's words, that it had let go of its first rule.

The *Obtwust* whirled. "Would an element dare speak against me!" The *spirit* cast a dark breath, and for a moment the fire was gone, save for an ember. Then the *Obtwust* released its hold, and the fire crawled back to life.

Fire was not deterred. "If you take my Keeper, you must take me, and then all the kin will die! And have you not just said, that a few kin would survive?"

The *Obtwust* flashed between anger and a dark laughter. The fire was clever and seemed to have caught the *Obtwust* in a trap. A fire could end its life. That power was given it and could not be taken away. Without fire, the kin would surely die this harsh winter, and if a few survived, the headhunters would take the rest.

The *Obtwust* challenged, "Would a fire extinguish itself for a human? Have you unlearned yourself? Perhaps you would become a human too?"

There was rustling not so far away. Fearsome Ones were creeping on the outskirts of their camp. Their eyes held a dark gleam, and their darkened teeth grinned. The *Obtwust,* who would broker no interruption, cast a finger that froze them.

It returned its attention to the Keepers, from whom it had so far withheld its force. The *Obtwust* had the power to do as it pleased, but it would not have its words undone. They were learning more.

Yet the spirit could not be so easily stopped, and its next words surprised Moeslet. "If Fire rises against me, if both Keepers resist me, maybe *all* the kin should be taken."

Could the Obtwust change its words after all? It seemed to say these things without the same insistence, however. That offered a little hope, for maybe the *Obtwust* could change so it would not take *any* lives. Or would it take them all? *If only the shaman were here, he would know what to do!*

There was a deep silence, more waiting, and Moeslet did not like the waiting. He hoped that more words could be found inside him, but none rose. They were stalemated. The *Obtwust* was waiting for something before it acted, and Moeslet had no clue what to do.

Tehmta did. She rose and stepped toward the fire.

"No!" cried Moeslet.

Tehmta did not hesitate. "The *Obtwust* wants me, and the fire would have me. How else can the kin be saved?"

She stepped into the fire.

The fire rose, blazing, and something unexpected happened. The fire burned around her, for the fire desired her, but Tehmta did not burn. She glowed as if she were a child of the flames.

Moeslet wondered how this could be possible. There was only one thing––the *Obtwust's* power must be surrounding her. This knowledge turned Moeslet's world upside down. - meant that the dark Spirit had the power to unmake the nature of fire itself. It meant that the *Obtwust* had been holding back all this time, making them think it could only take life. It had much more power, for it could hold back death. And if it had that much power, it was far greater than Moeslet had realized.

Moeslet did not know what to think or do, but he thought the *Obtwust* must still keep its word. One of them would die, and for some reason the *Obtwust* was protecting Tehmta.

Moeslet saw pain cross Tehmta's face, and they both felt the burning. The *Obtwust* had ceased to protect. But Moeslet had a life, and he tossed it her way. "Do not burn her! Release her," he ordered the fire. "You have promised me a life!"

Tehmta slowly stepped out, realizing she had failed. She passed out into Moeslet's arms, and he pulled her away from the fire.

Tehmta looked different, as if she was still glowing. Moeslet did not look up, but he sensed the *Obtwust* hovering over him. The dark Spirit would not be denied.

CHAPTER THIRTEEN
DAWN AND DEATH

THE *Obtwust* did not take Tehmta. She fell into a deep slumber and did not know the pain that followed. *Yes, this is the Obtwust's weakness. It likes strength, and she has shown great strength. True, she has become weak, but the Obtwust has passed over her. It is so like the night spirit that you can never tell what it will do next. Still, the Spirit of the Long Night will keep its word by taking one keeper, and it must be me.*

Moeslet knew he would die, but he would go down fighting. He would show the dark spirit that he was not a coward.

The *Obtwust's* hand, like a dark cocoon which nothing could penetrate, closed around him. All else was a blur, a whirlwind—and he was at the center.

"I am the Firekeeper. I have served the fire on many long nights. I will not die easily!"

The closing hand paused. Did the *Obtwust* want his agreement before taking him? Or was it trifling with him? "I know you will win, but I will fight you to the end!"

The *Obtwust* whirled, but in its whirling, it held back. Still, the little force it directed Moeslet's way, he could barely withstand, and he teetered toward death.

"Shaman spirit, help me!" Moeslet cried in the dark.

The spirit of the shaman obeyed, and it arose as a black jaguar. It attacked the *Obtwust*. The earth shuddered, but the *Obtwust* cast the jaguar away with a gesture, and the shaman spirit was gone.

Moeslet called on Fire. "I have nurtured you and kept you alive. Fight for me!"

The fire rose as if it would engulf the *Obtwust*. It would defend its old Keeper.

The Spirit of the Long Night seemed surprised. For a moment, it looked as if its dark hold would vanish, that the fire had burned it away. But the *Obtwust,* with a single breath, slapped it down to a few scattered coals.

These were all that Moeslet could think to summon. Before his feet lay the slumbering Tehmta; she had already done what she could do. The fire was struggling to come back. The shaman had disappeared.

Moeslet stood up, his back against the dying fire. He raised his fist at the invisible being. "Show yourself. Show yourself before you take me!"

The *Obtwust* flickered, for the dawn was coming. Had he somehow won? On this night when rules were broken?

Cries of alarm sounded; the headhunters were breaking through, flinging spears and stones. The kin had risen to drive them away and wounded were already falling. Moeslet was hit. So it was true, Moeslet thought, many will die. Maybe all, with the *Obtwust* content to watch. In anger, Moeslet looked towards the one who would let them die.

Moeslet had no other to call on, so he called upon the *Obtwust*. "Protect the kin, for you have said that some would not die. I heard you say the words—'only a few.' Then take me if you must."

It was a faint hope to call upon this deadly night spirit, and Moeslet closed his eyes, expecting all to end.

But the *Obtwust* listened, for the dark around Moeslet turned and lashed out toward the headhunters. It did not strike them with death, but with a terrible panic, and they fled.

So the kin survived this night, although many were left wounded, and Moeslet was dying. In dying, he had found the last secret of the Obtwust, that it would serve the kin. Just when Moeslet sensed the danger had passed, and that he wanted to tell the others what he had discovered—the Obtwust took him.

CHAPTER FOURTEEN
LET THE CHILD LIVE

TEHMTA WOKE. THE FIRE was scattered in places and wounded were lying all around. The attack had been cut short, and no kin had died save Moeslet.

"As it had said, the Spirit of the Long Night has taken a Keeper," Tehmta announced. The kin gathered around her, wondering what was meant.

The young shamaness credited Tehmta. "She summoned a fierce spirit that made the attackers flee. She is not only a Keeper but has shaman powers."

The others looked at this diminutive girl and saw little strength or power.

"Do not be deceived. I tell you what I saw," said the shamaness. "A spirit of great power took Moeslet. It must have listened to Tehmta. For it was upon the Spirit's command that the Headhunters scattered."

The day was dawning clear and bright. Leola had gone over to Moeslet's body and was weeping, cradling his head. The others did not weep, and as their fear lessened, their hunger grew.

There was a discussion about survival, as if the battle had already been forgotten. "Moeslet did not die in battle," said one. "He stood by the fire and received a blow. We have to cast bones for another life."

"This is no wound enough to have killed Moeslet," said Tehmta, puzzled. "He must have been slain by the Spirit."

"How do you know such things?" a kin asked. "You were asleep. You must have fallen into the fire too, for your feet are blackened. Still, we need not follow the old rules. Maybe he should become our food."

"No!" cried Leola, holding onto Moeslet. "The Keeper goes back to the fire. That is the rule of all Keepers."

The group wavered between their hunger and the rule.

The shamaness spoke. "Yes, a great spirit came, and somehow we have survived, save Moeslet. We must do as Leola has said and place him in the fire. We must trust that food will come another way, lest we anger the powerful Spirit that took him."

Despite their hunger, the kin would not go against the one who had been named shaman. So the hunters placed Moeslet in the fire, and his body burned.

It took a while before the body started burning however, the fire showing its last respect to its Keeper.

The next day, the hunters decided to cast bones, but food came in another way. A bear, awakened early from its winter hibernation, stumbled upon them. The hunters killed the still waking bear and fought off jackals who came later. Its flesh would be enough to sustain them for a few more days of the dark winter.

TWO MONTHS PASSED, and Leola's child was born. It had a game foot like Moeslet. The elders queried Leola, and she revealed she had lain with him.

There was a meeting of the Council who brought their stones of judgement. "The child should die on two counts," said the eldest. "He is not from the one who was given her, and he will not be a hunter. Why preserve such a one? We already have a Firekeeper." Two of the elders placed their burnt stones on the smooth rock.

The others of the Council were about to lie down their stones, but Tehmta rose to the child's defense. "Wait! There is more I have not told, something that should be kept secret among Keepers. But a life is at stake, so I must speak. Moeslet was the one who fought the night Spirit. This is a child of a great fighter."

The men of the Council laughed, for this was a great claim. When they looked to the shamaness and she did not object, they murmured.

Tehmta went on. "I know it came, for I was awake at first. It was fierce, wanting to take many, maybe all of us. We knew it would take one Keeper. I tried to go into the fire and have it take me, but the Spirit refused. I slept, it is true. That meant Moeslet was the only one left to face the spirit. Our shaman had already died, and the new shamaness, who had never faced such a spirit, was not here. Moeslet fought the dark Spirit, and it took him instead of me.

"The fight lasted until dawn, for the Spirit has a rule that it does not take in the day. So the Spirit passed us over. We *all* owe our lives to Moeslet!"

The Council talked among themselves, still gripping their black stones. Maybe it was so; maybe it wasn't. A great Spirit had come, and someone had battled the spirit. If it were Moeslet, they could not kill the child of the one to whom they owed their lives. For, if the child were to die by two counts, there were twenty or more by which he should live.

Leola spoke what they were thinking. "You must not kill the child of the one who received the blow of the *Obtwust* for us."

She spoke the name, for Moeslet had once revealed it to her on a summer day. Power in the air stirred at the name, and even those who knew nothing of spirit things sensed that a word of power had been spoken.

So the rest of the elders gave their word as they laid their unburnt stones on the rock.

One by one, all—even Leola's partner, declared, "Let the Child live."

The End

Did you love *The Firekeeper*? Then you should read *Child of the Elements*[1] by Michael A. Susko!

[2]

In the Pleistocene era, an "early child" was born to a mother, named Bough. Absent a male protector, Bough offers her child to the Elements. The fleeing mother also raises an abandoned girl, who can make partnerships with wolves. Kinder and Huntress are the future, but dangers abound from lions to half humans. Read this story if you would like to see how mothers, fierce in love and courage, birthed "New Ones" and became more fully human.

Read more at https://www.allroneofus.com/.

---

1. https://books2read.com/u/bzvRgn

2. https://books2read.com/u/bzvRgn

Also by Michael A. Susko

The Dreaming Series
Sleek Back
Streak and Cave Bear Dreaming
Moby and Marsupial Mole Dreaming

The Dream World Trilogy
Delphi, the Time Thief, and the Dream World
Detinna and the Cave God
The Resistance & the Empire

Worlds to the Side
Down Below and the Archon's Castle
Up Above and the Runaway
Across the Gulf and Journey Into Un-Time
On the Bay and a Wild Child Found
In the Wild and Do One Wild Thing
On the Mountain and Two Are Missing
To the Beginning and Journey Through Here

The Generation of LIfe: Imagery, Ritual and Experiences in Deep Caves
Alwon in Another World: An Archetypal Voyage
Line In the Wall
Twelve Suspects
2084
Gospel Characters

Watch for more at https://www.allroneofus.com/.

About the Author

The author has researched and lectured on the paleolithic era and shamanistic ritual/symbols of indigenous cultures throughout the world. In particular, his interests have led him to visit and photograph the indigenous of Guatemala, whose thatched homes and cave rituals make use of live fires. Last, he has published in evolution, showing how vulnerability is integral to increases in consciousness.

Read more at https://www.allroneofus.com/.